SELECTED POEMS

1956−1968

Books by Leonard Cohen

POETRY

Let Us Compare Mythologies (1956)
The Spice-Box of Earth (1961)
Flowers for Hitler (1964)
Parasites of Heaven (1966)

FICTION

The Favorite Game (1963)
Beautiful Losers (1966)

LEONARD COHEN

SELECTED POEMS

1956–1968

McClelland and Stewart Limited

Toronto/Montreal

Library of Congress catalog card number: 68–22317

Most of these poems were previously published
by McClelland and Stewart Limited in volumes
entitled *Let Us Compare Mythologies, The
Spice-Box of Earth, Flowers for Hitler,* and
Parasites of Heaven. "This Is for You" first ap-
peared in *Mademoiselle.* Other poems first ap-
peared in the *Queen's Quarterly, Prism, Saturday Review, Pan-ic, The McGill Chapbook,* and
Tamarack Review.

The Canadian Publishers
McClelland and Stewart Limited
25 Hollinger Road, Toronto 16

Printed in the U.S.A.

Fourth printing March 1969

Contents

I. *Let Us Compare Mythologies*

For Wilf and His House   *3*

Prayer for Messiah   *4*

The Song of the Hellenist   *5*

The Sparrows   *7*

City Christ   *8*

Song of Patience   *9*

When This American Woman   *10*

Song   *11*

These Heroics   *12*

Lovers   *13*

The Warrior Boats   *14*

Letter   *16*

Pagans   *18*

Song   *20*

Prayer for Sunset   *21*

Ballad   *23*

Saint Catherine Street   *24*

Ballad   *26*

Summer Night   *28*

The Flier   *29*

Poem   *30*

The Fly   *30*

Warning   *31*

Story   *32*

Beside the Shepherd   *33*

II. *The Spice-Box of Earth*

A Kite Is a Victim   *37*

The Flowers That I Left in the Ground   *38*

Gift   *39*

There Are Some Men   *40*

You All in White   *41*

I Wonder How Many People in This City   *42*

Go by Brooks   *43*

To a Teacher   *44*

I Have Not Lingered in European Monasteries   *45*

It Swings, Jocko   *46*

Credo   *48*

You Have the Lovers   *50*

Owning Everything   *52*

The Priest Says Goodbye   *54*

The Cuckold's Song   *56*

Dead Song   *57*

My Lady Can Sleep   *58*

Travel   *59*

I Have Two Bars of Soap   *60*

Celebration   *61*

Beneath My Hands   *62*

As the Mist Leaves No Scar   *63*

I Long to Hold Some Lady   *64*

Now of Sleeping   *65*

Song   *67*

Song   *68*

For Anne   *68*

Last Dance at the Four Penny   *69*

Summer Haiku   *70*

Out of the Land of Heaven   *71*

Prayer of My Wild Grandfather   72

Isaiah   73

The Genius   76

Lines from My Grandfather's Journal   78

III. *Flowers for Hitler*

What I'm Doing Here   87

The Hearth   88

The Drawer's Condition on November 28, 1961   89

The Suit   90

Indictment of the Blue Hole   91

I Wanted to Be a Doctor   92

On Hearing a Name Long Unspoken   93

Style   95

Goebbels Abandons His Novel and Joins the
    Party   97

Hitler the Brain-Mole   98

It Uses Us!   99

My Teacher Is Dying   100

For My Old Layton   102

Finally I Called   103

The Only Tourist in Havana Turns His Thoughts
    Homeward   104

Millennium   105

Alexander Trocchi, Public Junkie, Priez pour
    Nous   108

Three Good Nights   111

On the Sickness of My Love   113

For Marianne   114

The Failure of a Secular Life   115

My Mentors   116

Heirloom   *117*
The Project   *118*
Hydra 1963   *120*
All There Is to Know about Adolph Eichmann   *122*
The New Leader   *123*
For E.J.P.   *124*
A Migrating Dialogue   *125*
The Bus   *128*
The Rest Is Dross   *129*
How the Winter Gets In   *130*
Propaganda   *131*
Opium and Hitler   *132*
For Anyone Dressed in Marble   *134*
Folk   *134*
I Had It for a Moment   *135*
Independence   *137*
The House   *138*
The Lists   *139*
Order   *140*
Destiny   *142*
Queen Victoria and Me   *143*
The New Step: A Ballet-Drama in One Act   *145*
Winter Bulletin   *164*
Why Did You Give My Name to the Police?   *165*
The Music Crept by Us   *167*
Disguises   *168*
Lot   *171*
One of the Nights I Didn't Kill Myself   *172*
Bullets   *173*
The Big World   *174*
Front Lawn   *175*

Kerensky   *176*

Another Night with Telescope   *178*

IV. *Parasites of Heaven*

The Nightmares Do Not Suddenly   *181*

A Cross Didn't Fall on Me   *182*

So You're the Kind of Vegetarian   *183*

Nothing Has Been Broken   *184*

Here We Are at the Window   *185*

Clean as the Grass from Which   *186*

When I Paid the Sun to Run   *187*

I See You on a Greek Mattress   *188*

Suzanne Wears a Leather Coat   *189*

One Night I Burned the House I Loved   *190*

Two Went to Sleep   *191*

In the Bible Generations Pass . . .   *192*

Found Once Again Shamelessly Ignoring the
    Swans . . .   *193*

When I Hear You Sing   *194*

He Was Lame   *195*

I Am Too Loud When You Are Gone   *195*

Somewhere in My Trophy Room . . .   *196*

You Know Where I Have Been   *197*

I Met a Woman Long Ago   *198*

I've Seen Some Lonely History   *200*

Snow Is Falling   *201*

Created Fires I Cannot Love   *202*

Claim Me, Blood, If You Have a Story   *203*

He Was Beautiful When He Sat Alone   *204*

I Am a Priest of God   *207*

In Almond Trees Lemon Trees   *208*

Suzanne Takes You Down   209
Give Me Back My Fingerprints   211
Foreign God, Reigning in Earthly Glory . . .   213
I Believe You Heard Your Master Sing   214
This Morning I Was Dressed by the Wind   216
I Stepped into an Avalanche   217

V. *New Poems*

This Is for You   221
You Do Not Have to Love Me   223
It's Just a City, Darling   224
Edmonton, Alberta, December 1966, 4 a.m.   225
The Broom Is an Army of Straw   226
I Met You   227
Calm, Alone, the Cedar Guitar   228
You Live Like a God   229
Aren't You Tired   230
She Sings So Nice   231
The Reason I Write   231
When I Meet You in the Small Streets   232
It Has Been Some Time   233
A Person Who Eats Meat   233
Who Will Finally Say   234
Waiting to Tell the Doctor   235
It's Good to Sit with People   236
Do Not Forget Old Friends   238
Marita   239
He Studies to Describe   239

Index of First Lines   241

I / Let Us Compare Mythologies

FOR WILF AND HIS HOUSE

When young the Christians told me
how we pinned Jesus
like a lovely butterfly against the wood,
and I wept beside paintings of Calvary
at velvet wounds
and delicate twisted feet.

But he could not hang softly long,
your fighters so proud with bugles,
bending flowers with their silver stain,
and when I faced the Ark for counting,
trembling underneath the burning oil,
the meadow of running flesh turned sour
and I kissed away my gentle teachers,
warned my younger brothers.

Among the young and turning-great
of the large nations, innocent
of the spiked wish and the bright crusade,
there I could sing my heathen tears
between the summersaults and chestnut battles,
love the distant saint
who fed his arm to flies,
mourn the crushed ant
and despise the reason of the heel.

Raging and weeping are left on the early road.
Now each in his holy hill
the glittering and hurting days are almost done.
        Then let us compare mythologies.
I have learned my elaborate lie
of soaring crosses and poisoned thorns

and how my fathers nailed him
like a bat against a barn
to greet the autumn and late hungry ravens
as a hollow yellow sign.

PRAYER FOR MESSIAH

His blood on my arm is warm as a bird
his heart in my hand is heavy as lead
his eyes through my eyes shine brighter than love
O send out the raven ahead of the dove

His life in my mouth is less than a man
his death on my breast is harder than stone
his eyes through my eyes shine brighter than love
O send out the raven ahead of the dove

O send out the raven ahead of the dove
O sing from your chains where you're chained in a cave
your eyes through my eyes shine brighter than love
your blood in my ballad collapses the grave

O sing from your chains where you're chained in a cave
your eyes through my eyes shine brighter than love
your heart in my hand is heavy as lead
your blood on my arm is warm as a bird

O break from your branches a green branch of love
after the raven has died for the dove

THE SONG OF THE HELLENIST

(For R.K.)

> *Those unshadowed figures, rounded lines of men*
> *who kneel by curling waves, amused by ornate birds—*
> > *If that had been the ruling way,*
> *I would have grown long hairs for the corners of my*
> > > > > *mouth . . .*

O cities of the Decapolis across the Jordan,
you are too great; our young men love you,
and men in high places have caused gymnasiums
to be built in Jerusalem.
> I tell you, my people, the statues are too tall.
> Beside them we are small and ugly,
> blemishes on the pedestal.

My name is Theodotus, do not call me Jonathan.
My name is Dositheus, do not call me Nathaniel.
> Call us Alexander, Demetrius, Nicanor . . .

"Have you seen my landsmen in the museums,
the brilliant scholars with the dirty fingernails,
standing before the marble gods,
> underneath the lot?"
Among straight noses, natural and carved,
I have said my clever things thought out before;
jested on the Protocols, the cause of war,
> quoted "Bleistein with a Cigar."

And in the salon that holds the city in its great window,
in the salon among the Herrenmenschen,
among the close-haired youth, I made them laugh
when the child came in:

| 5

"Come, I need you for a Passover Cake."
And I have touched their tall clean women,
thinking somehow they are unclean,
    as scaleless fish.
They have smiled quietly at me,
and with their friends—
    I wonder what they see.

O cities of the Decapolis,
call us Alexander, Demetrius, Nicanor . . .
    Dark women, soon I will not love you.
My children will boast of their ancestors at Marathon
and under the walls of Troy,
    and Athens, my chiefest joy—

O call me Alexander, Demetrius, Nicanor . . .

THE SPARROWS

Catching winter in their carved nostrils
the traitor birds have deserted us,
leaving only the dullest brown sparrows
for spring negotiations.

I told you we were fools
to have them in our games,
but you replied:
        They are only wind-up birds
who strut on scarlet feet
so hopelessly far
from our curled fingers.

I had moved to warn you,
but you only adjusted your hair
and ventured:
        Their wings are made of glass and gold
and we are fortunate
not to hear them splintering
against the sun.

Now the hollow nests
sit like tumors or petrified blossoms
between the wire branches
and you, an innocent scientist,
question me on these brown sparrows:
whether we should plant our yards with breadcrumbs
or mark them with the black, persistent crows
whom we hate and stone.

But what shall I tell you of migrations
when in this empty sky

the precise ghosts of departed summer birds
still trace old signs;
or of desperate flights
when the dimmest flutter of a coloured wing
excites all our favourite streets
to delight in imaginary spring.

CITY CHRIST

He has returned from countless wars,
Blinded and hopelessly lame.
He endures the morning streetcars
And counts ages in a Peel Street room.

He is kept in his place like a court jew,
To consult on plagues or hurricanes,
And he never walks with them on the sea
Or joins their lonely sidewalk games.

SONG OF PATIENCE

For a lovely instant I thought she would grow mad
and end the reason's fever.
But in her hand she held Christ's splinter,
so I could only laugh and press a warm coin
across her seasoned breasts:
but I remembered clearly then your insane letters
and how you wove initials in my throat.

My friends warn me
that you have read the ocean's old skeleton;
they say you stitch the water sounds
in different mouths, in other monuments.
"Journey with a silver bullet," they caution.
"Conceal a stake inside your pocket."
And I must smile as they misconstrue your insane letters
and my embroidered throat.

O I will tell him to love you carefully;
to honour you with shells and coloured bottles;
to keep from your face the falling sand
and from your human arm the time-charred beetle;
to teach you new stories about lightning
and let you run sometimes barefoot on the shore.
And when the needle grins bloodlessly in his cheek
he will come to know how beautiful it is
to be loved by a madwoman.

And I do not gladly wait the years
for the ocean to discover and rust your face
as it has all of history's beacons
that have turned their gold and stone to water's onslaught,

for then your letters too rot with ocean's logic
and my fingernails are long enough
to tear the stitches from my throat.

WHEN THIS AMERICAN WOMAN

When this American woman,
whose thighs are bound in casual red cloth,
comes thundering past my sitting-place
like a forest-burning Mongol tribe,
the city is ravished
and brittle buildings of a hundred years
splash into the street;
and my eyes are burnt
for the embroidered Chinese girls,
already old,
and so small between the thin pines
on these enormous landscapes,
that if you turn your head
they are lost for hours.

SONG

The naked weeping girl
is thinking of my name
turning my bronze name
over and over
with the thousand fingers
of her body
anointing her shoulders
with the remembered odour
of my skin

O I am the general
in her history
over the fields
driving the great horses
dressed in gold cloth
wind on my breastplate
sun in my belly

May soft birds
soft as a story to her eyes
protect her face
from my enemies
and vicious birds
whose sharp wings
were forged in metal oceans
guard her room
from my assassins

And night deal gently with her
high stars maintain the whiteness
of her uncovered flesh

And may my bronze name
touch always her thousand fingers
grow brighter with her weeping
until I am fixed like a galaxy
and memorized
in her secret and fragile skies.

THESE HEROICS

If I had a shining head
and people turned to stare at me
in the streetcars;
and I could stretch my body
through the bright water
and keep abreast of fish and water snakes;
if I could ruin my feathers
in flight before the sun;
do you think that I would remain in this room,
reciting poems to you,
and making outrageous dreams
with the smallest movements of your mouth?

LOVERS

During the first pogrom they
Met behind the ruins of their homes—
Sweet merchants trading: her love
For a history-full of poems.

And at the hot ovens they
Cunningly managed a brief
Kiss before the soldier came
To knock out her golden teeth.

And in the furnace itself
As the flames flamed higher,
He tried to kiss her burning breasts
As she burned in the fire.

Later he often wondered:
Was their barter completed?
While men around him plundered
And knew he had been cheated.

THE WARRIOR BOATS

The warrior boats from Portugal
Strain at piers with ribs exposed
And seagull generations fall
Through the wood anatomy

But in the town, the town
Their passion unimpaired
The beautiful dead crewmen
Go climbing in the lanes
Boasting poems and bitten coins

Handsome bastards
What do they care
If the Empire has withered
To half a peninsula
If the Queen has the King's Adviser
For her last and seventh lover

Their maps have not changed
Thighs still are white and warm
New boundaries have not altered
The marvellous landscape of bosoms
Nor a Congress relegated the red mouth
To a foreign district

Then let the ships disintegrate
At the edge of the land
The gulls will find another place to die
Let the home ports put on mourning

And little clerks
Complete the necessary papers

But you swagger on, my enemy sailors
Go climbing in the lanes
Boasting your poems and bitten coins
Go knocking on all the windows of the town

At one place you will find my love
Asleep and waiting
And I cannot know how long
She has dreamed of all of you

Oh remove my coat gently
From her shoulders.

LETTER

How you murdered your family
means nothing to me
as your mouth moves across my body

And I know your dreams
of crumbling cities and galloping horses
of the sun coming too close
and the night never ending

but these mean nothing to me
beside your body

I know that outside a war is raging
that you issue orders
that babies are smothered and generals beheaded

but blood means nothing to me
it does not disturb your flesh

tasting blood on your tongue
does not shock me
as my arms grow into your hair

Do not think I do not understand
what happens
after the troops have been massacred
and the harlots put to the sword

And I write this only to rob you

that when one morning my head
hangs dripping with the other generals
from your house gate

that all this was anticipated
and so you will know that it meant nothing to me.

PAGANS

With all Greek heroes
swarming around my shoulders,
I perverted the Golem formula
and fashioned you from grass,
using oaths of cruel children
for my father's chant.

O pass by, I challenged you
and gods in their approval
rustled my hair with marble hands,
and you approached slowly
with all the pain of a thousand-year statue
breaking into life.

I thought you perished
at our first touch
(for in my hand I held a fragment
of a French cathedral
and in the air a man spoke to birds
and everywhere
the dangerous smell of old Italian flesh).

But yesterday while children
slew each other in a dozen games,
I heard you wandering through grass
and watched you glare (O Dante)
where I had stood.

I know how our coarse grass
mutilates your feet,
    how the city traffic
echoes all his sonnets

and how you lean for hours
at the cemetery gates.

Dear friend, I have searched all night
    through each burnt paper,
but I fear I will never find
the formula to let you die.

SONG

My lover Peterson
He named me Goldenmouth
I changed him to a bird
And he migrated south

My lover Frederick
Wrote sonnets to my breast
I changed him to a horse
And he galloped west

My lover Levite
He named me Bitterfeast
I changed him to a serpent
And he wriggled east

My lover I forget
He named me Death
I changed him to a catfish
And he swam north

My lover I imagine
He cannot form a name
I'll nestle in his fur
And never be to blame.

PRAYER FOR SUNSET

The sun is tangled
    in black branches,
raving like Absalom
    between sky and water,
struggling through the dark terebinth
to commit its daily suicide.

Now, slowly, the sea consumes it,
leaving a glistening wound
    on the water,
    a red scar on the horizon;
In darkness
    I set out for home,
terrified by the clash of wind on grass,
and the victory cry of weeds and water.

Is there no Joab for tomorrow night,
    with three darts
    and a great heap of stones?

BALLAD

He pulled a flower
out of the moss
and struggled past soldiers
to stand at the cross.

He dipped the flower
into a wound
and hoped that a garden
would grow in his hand.

The hanging man shivered
at this gentle thrust
and ripped his flesh
from the flower's touch,

and said in a voice
they had not heard,
"Will petals find roots
in the wounds where I bleed?

"Will minstrels learn songs
from a tongue which is torn
and sick be made whole
through rents in my skin?"

The people knew something
like a god had spoken
and stared with fear
at the nails they had driven.

And they fell on the man
with spear and knife

to honour the voice
with a sacrifice.

O the hanging man
had words for the crowd
but he was tired
and the prayers were loud.

He thought of islands
alone in the sea
and sea water bathing
dark roots of each tree;

of tidal waves lunging
over the land,
over these crosses
these hills and this man.

He thought of towns
and fields of wheat,
of men and this man
but he could not speak.

O they hid two bodies
behind a stone;
day became night
and the crowd went home.

And men from Golgotha
assure me that still
gardeners in vain
pour blood in that soil.

SAINT CATHERINE STREET

Towering black nuns frighten us
as they come lumbering down the tramway aisle
amulets and talismans caught in careful fingers
promising plagues for an imprudent glance
So we bow our places away
       the price of an indulgence

How may we be saints and live in golden coffins
Who will leave on our stone shelves
       pathetic notes for intervention
How may we be calm marble gods at ocean altars
Who will murder us for some high reason

There are no ordeals
Fire and water have passed from the wizards' hands
We cannot torture or be tortured
Our eyes are worthless to an inquisitor's heel
No prince will waste hot lead
       or build a spiked casket for us

Once with a flaming belly she danced upon a green road
Move your hand slowly through a cobweb
       and make drifting strings for puppets
Now the tambourines are dull
at her lifted skirt boys study cigarette stubs
no one is jealous of her body

We would bathe in a free river
but the lepers in some spiteful gesture
have suicided in the water

and all the swollen quiet bodies crowd the other
    prey for a fearless thief or beggar

How can we love and pray
when at our lovers' arms
we hear the damp bells of them
who once took bitter alms
but now float quietly away

Will no one carve from our bodies a white cross
for a wind-torn mountain
or was that forsaken man's pain
enough to end all passion

Are those dry faces and hands we see
all the flesh there is of nuns
Are they really clever non-excreting tapestries
prepared by skillful eunuchs
for our trembling friends

BALLAD

My lady was found mutilated
in a Mountain Street boarding house.
My lady was a tall slender love,
    like one of Tennyson's girls,
and you always imagined her erect on a thoroughbred
in someone's private forest.
    But there she was,
naked on an old bed, knife slashes
across her breasts, legs badly cut up:
Dead two days.

They promised me an early conviction.
We will eavesdrop on the adolescents
    examining pocket-book covers in drugstores.
We will note the broadest smiles at torture scenes
    in movie houses.
We will watch the old men in Dominion Square
    follow with their eyes
the secretaries from the Sun Life at five-thirty . . .

Perhaps the tabloids alarmed him.
Whoever he was the young man came alone
    to see the frightened blonde have her blouse
ripped away by anonymous hands;
the person guarded his mouth
    who saw the poker blacken the eyes
of the Roman prisoner;
the old man pretended to wind his pocket-watch . . .

The man was never discovered.
There are so many cities!
    so many knew of my lady and her beauty.

Perhaps he came from Toronto, a half-crazed man
    looking for some Sunday love;
or a vicious poet stranded too long in Winnipeg;
or a Nova Scotian fleeing from the rocks and preachers . . .

Everyone knew my lady
    from the movies and art-galleries,
Body from Goldwyn. Botticelli had drawn her long limbs.
Rossetti the full mouth.
Ingres had coloured her skin.
    She should not have walked so bravely
through the streets.
After all, that was the Marian year, the year
the rabbis emerged from their desert exile, the year
the people were inflamed by tooth-paste ads . . .

We buried her in Spring-time.
    The sparrows in the air
wept that we should hide with earth
    the face of one so fair.

The flowers they were roses
    and such sweet fragrance gave
that all my friends were lovers
    and we danced upon her grave.

SUMMER NIGHT

The moon dangling wet like a half-plucked eye
was bright for my friends bred in close avenues
of stone, and let us see too much.
The vast treeless field and huge wounded sky,
opposing each other like continents,
made us and our smoking fire quite irrelevant
between their eternal attitudes.
We knew we were intruders. Worse. Intruders
unnoticed and undespised.

     Through orchards of black weeds
with a sigh the river urged its silver flesh.
From their damp nests bull-frogs croaked
warnings, but to each other.
And occasional birds, in a private grudge,
flew noiselessly at the moon.
What could we do? We ran naked into the river,
but our flesh insulted the thick slow water.
We tried to sit naked on the stones,
but they were cold and we soon dressed.
One squeezed a little human music from his box:
mostly it was lost in the grass
where one struggled in an ignorant embrace.
One argued with the slight old hills
and the goose-fleshed naked girls, I will not be old.
One, for his protest, registered a sexual groan.
And the girl in my arms
broke suddenly away, and shouted for us all,
Help! Help! I am alone. But then all subtlety was gone
and it was stupid to be obvious before the field and sky,
experts in simplicity. So we fled on the highways,
in our armoured cars, back to air-conditioned homes.

THE FLIER

Do not arrange your bright flesh in the sun
Or shine your limbs, my love, toward this height
Where basket men and the lame must run, must run
And grasp at angels in their lovely flight
With stumps and hooks and artificial skin.
O there is nothing in your body's light
To grow us wings or teach the discipline
Which starvers know to calm the appetite.
Understand we might be content to beg
The clinic of your thighs against the night
Were there no scars of braces on his leg
Who sings and wrestles with them in our sight,
Then climbs the sky, a lover in their band.
Tell him your warmth, show him your gleaming hand.

POEM

I heard of a man
who says words so beautifully
that if he only speaks their name
women give themselves to him.

If I am dumb beside your body
while silence blossoms like tumors on our lips
it is because I hear a man climb stairs
and clear his throat outside our door.

THE FLY

In his black armour
    the house-fly marched the field
of Freia's sleeping thighs,
undisturbed by the soft hand
    which vaguely moved
to end his exercise.

And it ruined my day—
    this fly which never planned
to charm her or to please
should walk boldly on that ground
    I tried so hard
to lay my trembling knees.

WARNING

If your neighbour disappears
O if your neighbour disappears
The quiet man who raked his lawn
The girl who always took the sun

Never mention it to your wife
Never say at dinner time
Whatever happened to that man
Who used to rake his lawn

Never say to your daughter
As you're walking home from church
Funny thing about that girl
I haven't seen her for a month

And if your son says to you
Nobody lives next door
They've all gone away
Send him to bed with no supper

Because it can spread, it can spread
And one fine evening coming home
Your wife and daughter and son
They'll have caught the idea and will be gone.

STORY

She tells me a child built her house
one Spring afternoon,
but that the child was killed
crossing the street.

She says she read it in the newspaper,
that at the corner of this and this avenue
a child was run down by an automobile.

Of course I do not believe her.
She has built the house herself,
hung the oranges and coloured beads in the doorways,
crayoned flowers on the walls.
She has made the paper things for the wind,
collected crooked stones for their shadows in the sun,
fastened yellow and dark balloons to the ceiling.

Each time I visit her
she repeats the story of the child to me,
I never question her. It is important
to understand one's part in a legend.

I take my place
among the paper fish and make-believe clocks,
naming the flowers she has drawn,
smiling while she paints my head on large clay coins,
and making a sort of courtly love to her
when she contemplates her own traffic death.

BESIDE THE SHEPHERD

Beside the shepherd dreams the beast
Of laying down with lions.
The youth puts away his singing reed
And strokes the consecrated flesh.

Glory, Glory, shouts the grass,
Shouts the brick, as from the cliff
The gorgeous fallen sun
Rolls slowly on the promised city.

Naked running through the mansion
The boy with news of the Messiah
Forgets the message for his father,
Enjoying the marble against his feet.

Well finally it has happened,
Imagines someone in another house,
Staring one more minute out his window
Before waking up his wife.

II / The Spice-Box of Earth

A KITE IS A VICTIM

A kite is a victim you are sure of.
You love it because it pulls
gentle enough to call you **master**,
strong enough to call you fool;
because it lives
like a desperate trained falcon
in the high sweet air,
and you can always haul it down
to tame it in your drawer.

A kite is a fish you have already caught
in a pool where no fish come,
so you play him carefully and long,
and hope he won't give up,
or the wind die down.

A kite is the last poem you've written,
so you give it to the wind,
but you don't let it go
until someone finds you
something else to do.

A kite is a contract of glory
that must be made with the sun,
so you make friends with the field
the river and the wind,
then you pray the whole cold night before,
under the travelling cordless moon,
to make you worthy and lyric and pure.

THE FLOWERS THAT I LEFT
IN THE GROUND

The flowers that I left in the ground,
that I did not gather for you,
today I bring them all back,
to let them grow forever,
not in poems or marble,
but where they fell and rotted.

And the ships in their great stalls,
huge and transitory as heroes,
ships I could not captain,
today I bring them back
to let them sail forever,
not in model or ballad,
but where they were wrecked and scuttled.

And the child on whose shoulders I stand,
whose longing I purged
with public, kingly discipline,
today I bring him back
to languish forever,
not in confession or biography,
but where he flourished,
growing sly and hairy.

It is not malice that draws me away,
draws me to renunciation, betrayal:
it is weariness, I go for weariness of thee.
Gold, ivory, flesh, love, God, blood, moon—
I have become the expert of the catalogue.

My body once so familiar with glory,
my body has become a museum:
this part remembered because of someone's mouth,
this because of a hand,
this of wetness, this of heat.

Who owns anything he has not made?
With your beauty I am as uninvolved
as with horses' manes and waterfalls.
This is my last catalogue.
I breathe the breathless
I love you, I love you—
and let you move forever.

GIFT

You tell me that silence
is nearer to peace than poems
but if for my gift
I brought you silence
 (for I know silence)
you would say
This is not silence
this is another poem
and you would hand it back to me.

THERE ARE SOME MEN

There are some men
who should have mountains
to bear their names to time.

Grave-markers are not high enough
or green,
and sons go far away
to lose the fist
their father's hand will always seem.

I had a friend:
he lived and died in mighty silence
and with dignity,
left no book, son, or lover to mourn.

Nor is this a mourning-song
but only a naming of this mountain
on which I walk,
fragrant, dark, and softly white
under the pale of mist.
I name this mountain after him.

YOU ALL IN WHITE

Whatever cities are brought down,
I will always bring you poems,
and the fruit of orchards
I pass by.

Strangers in your bed,
excluded by our grief,
listening to sleep-whispering,
will hear their passion beautifully explained,
and weep because they cannot kiss
your distant face.

Lovers of my beloved,
watch how my words put on her lips like clothes,
how they wear her body like a rare shawl.
Fruit is pyramided on the window-sill,
songs flutter against the disappearing wall.

The sky of the city
is washed in the fire
of Lebanese cedar and gold.
In smoky filigree cages
the apes and peacocks fret.
Now the cages do not hold,
in the burning street man and animal
perish in each other's arms,
peacocks drown around the melting throne.

Is it the king
who lies beside you listening?
Is it Solomon or David
or stuttering Charlemagne?

Is that his crown
in the suitcase beside your bed?

When we meet again,
you all in white,
I smelling of orchards,
when we meet—

But now you awaken,
and you are tired of this dream.
Turn toward the sad-eyed man.
He stayed by you all the night.
You will have something
to say to him.

I WONDER HOW MANY PEOPLE
IN THIS CITY

I wonder how many people in this city
live in furnished rooms.
Late at night when I look out at the buildings
I swear I see a face in every window
looking back at me,
and when I turn away
I wonder how many go back to their desks
and write this down.

GO BY BROOKS

Go by brooks, love,
Where fish stare,
Go by brooks,
I will pass there.

Go by rivers,
Where eels throng,
Rivers, love,
I won't be long.

Go by oceans,
Where whales sail,
Oceans, love,
I will not fail.

TO A TEACHER

Hurt once and for all into silence.
A long pain ending without a song to prove it.

Who could stand beside you so close to Eden,
when you glinted in every eye the held-high razor,
shivering every ram and son?

And now the silent loony-bin,
where the shadows live in the rafters
like day-weary bats,
until the turning mind, a radar signal,
lures them to exaggerate mountain-size
on the white stone wall
your tiny limp.

How can I leave you in such a house?
Are there no more saints and wizards
to praise their ways with pupils,
no more evil to stun with the slap
of a wet red tongue?

Did you confuse the Messiah in a mirror
and rest because he had finally come?

Let me cry Help beside you, Teacher.
I have entered under this dark roof
as fearlessly as an honoured son
enters his father's house.

I HAVE NOT LINGERED IN
EUROPEAN MONASTERIES

I have not lingered in European monasteries
and discovered among the tall grasses tombs of knights
who fell as beautifully as their ballads tell;
I have not parted the grasses
or purposefully left them thatched.

I have not released my mind to wander and wait
in those great distances
between the snowy mountains and the fishermen,
like a moon,
or a shell beneath the moving water.

I have not held my breath
so that I might hear the breathing of God,
or tamed my heartbeat with an exercise,
or starved for visions.
Although I have watched him often
I have not become the heron,
leaving my body on the shore,
and I have not become the luminous trout,
leaving my body in the air.

I have not worshipped wounds and relics,
or combs of iron,
or bodies wrapped and burnt in scrolls.

I have not been unhappy for ten thousand years.
During the day I laugh and during the night I sleep.
My favourite cooks prepare my meals,
my body cleans and repairs itself,
and all my work goes well.

It swings, Jocko,
but we do not want too much flesh in it.
Make it like fifteenth-century prayers,
love with no climax,
constant love,
and passion without flesh.
(Draw those out, Jocko,
like the long snake from Moses' arm;
how he must have screamed
to see a snake come out of him;
no wonder he never felt holy:
We want that scream tonight.)
Lightly, lightly,
I want to be hungry,
hungry for food,
for love, for flesh;
I want my dreams to be of deprivation,
gold thorns being drawn from my temples.
If I am hungry
then I am great,
and I love like the passionate scientist
who knows the sky
is made only of wave-lengths.
Now if you want to stand up,
stand up lightly,
we'll lightly march around the city.
I'm behind you, man,
and the streets are spread with chicks and palms,
white branches and summer arms.
We're going through on tiptoe,
like monks before the Virgin's statue.

We built the city,
we drew the water through,
we hang around the rinks,
the bars, the festive halls,
like Brueghel's men.
Hungry, hungry.
Come back, Jocko,
bring it all back for the people here,
it's your turn now.

CREDO

A cloud of grasshoppers
rose from where we loved
and passed before the sun.

I wondered what farms
they would devour,
what slave people would go free
because of them.

I thought of pyramids overturned,
of Pharaoh hanging by the feet,
his body smeared—

Then my love drew me down
to conclude what I had begun.

Later, clusters of fern apart,
we lay.

A cloud of grasshoppers
passed between us and the moon,
going the other way,

each one fat and flying slow,
not hungry for the leaves and ferns
we rested on below.

The smell that burning cities give
was in the air.

Battalions of the wretched,
wild with holy promises,
soon passed our sleeping place;

they ran among
the ferns and grass.

I had two thoughts:
to leave my love
and join their wandering,

join their holiness;
    or take my love
to the city they had fled:
    That impoverished world
of boil-afflicted flesh
and rotting fields
could not tempt us from each other.

    Our ordinary morning lust
claimed my body first
and made me sane.
    I must not betray
the small oasis where we lie,
though only for a time.
    It is good to live between
a ruined house of bondage
and a holy promised land.
    A cloud of grasshoppers
will turn another Pharaoh upside-down;
slaves will build cathedrals
for other slaves to burn.
    It is good to hear
the larvae rumbling underground,
good to learn
the feet of fierce or humble priests
trample out the green.

YOU HAVE THE LOVERS

You have the lovers,
they are nameless, their histories only for each other,
and you have the room, the bed and the windows.
Pretend it is a ritual.
Unfurl the bed, bury the lovers, blacken the windows,
let them live in that house for a generation or two.
No one dares disturb them.
Visitors in the corridor tip-toe past the long closed door,
they listen for sounds, for a moan, for a song:
nothing is heard, not even breathing.
You know they are not dead,
you can feel the presence of their intense love.
Your children grow up, they leave you,
they have become soldiers and riders.
Your mate dies after a life of service.
Who knows you? Who remembers you?
But in your house a ritual is in progress:
it is not finished: it needs more people.
One day the door is opened to the lover's chamber.
The room has become a dense garden,
full of colours, smells, sounds you have never known.
The bed is smooth as a wafer of sunlight,
in the midst of the garden it stands alone.
In the bed the lovers, slowly and deliberately and silently,
perform the act of love.
Their eyes are closed,
as tightly as if heavy coins of flesh lay on them.
Their lips are bruised with new and old bruises.
Her hair and his beard are hopelessly tangled.
When he puts his mouth against her shoulder
she is uncertain whether her shoulder
has given or received the kiss.

All her flesh is like a mouth.
He carries his fingers along her waist
and feels his own waist caressed.
She holds him closer and his own arms tighten around her.
She kisses the hand beside her mouth.
It is his hand or her hand, it hardly matters,
there are so many more kisses.
You stand beside the bed, weeping with happiness,
you carefully peel away the sheets
from the slow-moving bodies.
Your eyes are filled with tears, you barely make out the
    lovers.
As you undress you sing out, and your voice is magnificent
because now you believe it is the first human voice
heard in that room.
The garments you let fall grow into vines.
You climb into bed and recover the flesh.
You close your eyes and allow them to be sewn shut.
You create an embrace and fall into it.
There is only one moment of pain or doubt
as you wonder how many multitudes are lying beside your
    body,
but a mouth kisses and a hand soothes the moment away.

OWNING EVERYTHING

For your sake I said I will praise the moon,
tell the colour of the river,
find new words for the agony
and ecstasy of gulls.

Because you are close,
everything that men make, observe
or plant is close, is mine:
the gulls slowly writhing, slowly singing
on the spears of wind;
the iron gate above the river;
the bridge holding between stone fingers
her cold bright necklace of pearls.

The branches of shore trees,
like trembling charts of rivers,
call the moon for an ally
to claim their sharp journeys
out of the dark sky,
but nothing in the sky responds.
The branches only give a sound
to miles of wind.

With your body and your speaking
you have spoken for everything,
robbed me of my strangerhood,
made me one
with the root and gull and stone,
and because I sleep so near to you
I cannot embrace
or have my private love with them.

You worry that I will leave you.
I will not leave you.
Only strangers travel.
Owning everything,
I have nowhere to go.

THE PRIEST SAYS GOODBYE

My love, the song is less than sung
when with your lips you take it from my tongue—
nor can you seize this firm erotic grace
and halt it tumbling into commonplace.

No one I know can set the hook
to fix lust in a longing look
where we can read from time to time
the absolute ballet our bodies mime.

Harry can't, his face in Sally's crotch,
nor Tom, who only loves when neighbours watch—
one mistakes the ballet for the chart,
one hopes that gossip will perform like art.

And what of art? When passion dies
friendship hovers round our flesh like flies,
and we name beautiful the smells
that corpses give and immortelles.

I have studied rivers: the waters rush
like eternal fire in Moses' bush.
Some things live with honour. I will see
lust burn like fire in a holy tree.

Do not come with me. When I stand alone
my voice sings out as though I did not own
my throat. Abelard proved how bright could be
the bed between the hermitage and nunnery.

You are beautiful. I will sing beside
rivers where longing Hebrews cried.

As separate exiles we can learn
how desert trees ignite and branches burn.

At certain crossroads we will win
the harvest of our discipline.
Swollen flesh, minds fed on wilderness—
Oh, what a blaze of love our bodies press!

THE CUCKOLD'S SONG

If this looks like a poem
I might as well warn you at the beginning
that it's not meant to be one.
I don't want to turn anything into poetry.
I know all about her part in it
but I'm not concerned with that right now.
This is between you and me.
Personally I don't give a damn who led who on:
in fact I wonder if I give a damn at all.
But a man's got to say something.
Anyhow you fed her 5 McKewan Ales,
took her to your room, put the right records on,
and in an hour or two it was done.
I know all about passion and honour
but unfortunately this had really nothing to do with
        either:
oh there was passion I'm only too sure
and even a little honour
but the important thing was to cuckold Leonard Cohen.
Hell, I might just as well address this to the both of you:
I haven't time to write anything else.
I've got to say my prayers.
I've got to wait by the window.
I repeat: the important thing was to cuckold Leonard
        Cohen.
I like that line because it's got my name in it.
What really makes me sick
is that everything goes on as it went before:
I'm still a sort of friend,
I'm still a sort of lover.
But not for long:
that's why I'm telling this to the two of you.

The fact is I'm turning to gold, turning to gold.
It's a long process, they say,
it happens in stages.
This is to inform you that I've already turned to clay.

DEAD SONG

As I lay dead
In my love-soaked bed,
Angels came to kiss my head.

I caught one gown
And wrestled her down
To be my girl in death town.

She will not fly.
She has promised to die.
What a clever corpse am I!

MY LADY CAN SLEEP

My lady can sleep
Upon a handkerchief
Or if it be Fall
Upon a fallen leaf.

I have seen the hunters
Kneel before her hem—
Even in her sleep
She turns away from them.

The only gift they offer
Is their abiding grief—
I pull out my pockets
For a handkerchief or leaf.

TRAVEL

Loving you, flesh to flesh, I often thought
Of travelling penniless to some mud throne
Where a master might instruct me how to plot
My life away from pain, to love alone
In the bruiseless embrace of stone and lake.

Lost in the fields of your hair I was never lost
Enough to lose a way I had to take;
Breathless beside your body I could not exhaust
The will that forbid me contract, vow,
Or promise, and often while you slept
I looked in awe beyond your beauty.

                          Now
I know why many men have stopped and wept
Half-way between the loves they leave and seek,
And wondered if travel leads them anywhere—
Horizons keep the soft line of your cheek,
The windy sky's a locket for your hair.

I have two bars of soap,
the fragrance of almond,
one for you and one for me.
Draw the bath,
we will wash each other.

I have no money,
I murdered the pharmacist.

And here's a jar of oil,
just like in the Bible.
Lie in my arms,
I'll make your flesh glisten.

I have no money,
I murdered the perfumer.

Look through the window
at the shops and people.
Tell me what you desire,
you'll have it by the hour.

I have no money,
I have no money.

CELEBRATION

When you kneel below me
and in both your hands
hold my manhood like a sceptre,

When you wrap your tongue
about the amber jewel
and urge my blessing,

I understand those Roman girls
who danced around a shaft of stone
and kissed it till the stone was warm.

Kneel, love, a thousand feet below me,
so far I can barely see your mouth and hands
perform the ceremony,

Kneel till I topple to your back
with a groan, like those gods on the roof
that Samson pulled down.

BENEATH MY HANDS

Beneath my hands
your small breasts
are the upturned bellies
of breathing fallen sparrows.

Wherever you move
I hear the sounds of closing wings
of falling wings.

I am speechless
because you have fallen beside me
because your eyelashes
are the spines of tiny fragile animals.

I dread the time
when your mouth
begins to call me hunter.

When you call me close
to tell me
your body is not beautiful
I want to summon
the eyes and hidden mouths
of stone and light and water
to testify against you.

I want them
to surrender before you
the trembling rhyme of your face
from their deep caskets.

When you call me close
to tell me

your body is not beautiful
I want my body and my hands
to be pools
for your looking and laughing.

AS THE MIST LEAVES NO SCAR

As the mist leaves no scar
On the dark green hill,
So my body leaves no scar
On you, nor ever will.

When wind and hawk encounter,
What remains to keep?
So you and I encounter,
Then turn, then fall to sleep.

As many nights endure
Without a moon or star,
So will we endure
When one is gone and far.

I LONG TO HOLD SOME LADY

I long to hold some lady
For my love is far away,
And will not come tomorrow
And was not here today.

There is no flesh so perfect
As on my lady's bone,
And yet it seems so distant
When I am all alone:

As though she were a masterpiece
In some castled town,
That pilgrims come to visit
And priests to copy down.

Alas, I cannot travel
To a love I have so deep
Or sleep too close beside
A love I want to keep.

But I long to hold some lady,
For flesh is warm and sweet.
Cold skeletons go marching
Each night beside my feet.

NOW OF SLEEPING

Under her grandmother's patchwork quilt
a calico bird's-eye view
of crops and boundaries
naming dimly the districts of her body
sleeps my Annie like a perfect lady

Like ages of weightless snow
on tiny oceans filled with light
her eyelids enclose deeply
a shade tree of birthday candles
one for every morning
until the now of sleeping

The small banner of blood
kept and flown by Brother Wind
long after the pierced bird fell down
is like her red mouth
among the squalls of pillow

Bearers of evil fancy
of dark intention and corrupting fashion
who come to rend the quilt
plough the eye and ground the mouth
will contend with mighty Mother Goose
and Farmer Brown and all good stories
of invincible belief
which surround her sleep
like the golden weather of a halo

Well-wishers and her true lover
may stay to watch my Annie
sleeping like a perfect lady

under her grandmother's patchwork quilt
but they must promise to whisper
and to vanish by morning—
all but her one true lover.

SONG

When with lust I am smitten
To my books I then repair
And read what men have written
Of flesh forbid but fair

But in these saintly stories
Of gleaming thigh and breast
Of sainthood and its glories
Alas I find no rest

For at each body rare
The saintly man disdains
I stare O God I stare
My heart is stained with stains

And casting down the holy tomes
I lead my eyes to where
The naked girls with silver combs
Are combing out their hair

Then each pain my hermits sing
Flies upward like a spark
I live with the mortal ring
Of flesh on flesh in dark

SONG

I almost went to bed
without remembering
the four white violets
I put in the button-hole
of your green sweater

and how I kissed you then
and you kissed me
shy as though I'd
never been your lover

FOR ANNE

With Annie gone,
Whose eyes to compare
With the morning sun?

Not that I did compare,
But I do compare
Now that she's gone.

LAST DANCE AT THE FOUR PENNY

Layton, when we dance our freilach
under the ghostly handkerchief,
the miracle rabbis of Prague and Vilna
resume their sawdust thrones,
and angels and men, asleep so long
in the cold palaces of disbelief,
gather in sausage-hung kitchens
to quarrel deliciously and debate
the sounds of the Ineffable Name.

Layton, my friend Lazarovitch,
no Jew was ever lost
while we two dance joyously
in this French province,
cold and oceans west of the temple,
the snow canyoned on the twigs
like forbidden Sabbath manna;
I say no Jew was ever lost
while we weave and billow the handkerchief
into a burning cloud,
measuring all of heaven
with our stitching thumbs.

Reb Israel Lazarovitch,
you no-good Romanian, you're right!
Who cares whether or not
the Messiah is a Litvak?
As for the cynical,
such as we were yesterday,
let them step with us or rot
in their logical shrouds.
We've raised a bright white flag,

and here's our battered fathers' cup of wine,
and now is music
until morning and the morning prayers
lay us down again,
we who dance so beautifully
though we know that freilachs end.

SUMMER HAIKU

For Frank and Marian Scott

Silence

and a deeper silence

when the crickets

hesitate

OUT OF THE LAND OF HEAVEN

For Marc Chagall

Out of the land of heaven
Down comes the warm Sabbath sun
Into the spice-box of earth.
The Queen will make every Jew her lover.
    In a white silk coat
Our rabbi dances up the street,
Wearing our lawns like a green prayer-shawl,
Brandishing houses like silver flags.
    Behind him dance his pupils,
Dancing not so high
And chanting the rabbi's prayer,
But not so sweet.
    And who waits for him
On a throne at the end of the street
But the Sabbath Queen.
    Down go his hands
Into the spice-box of earth,
And there he finds the fragrant sun
For a wedding ring,
And draws her wedding finger through.
    Now back down the street they go,
Dancing higher than the silver flags.
His pupils somewhere have found wives too,
And all are chanting the rabbi's song
And leaping high in the perfumed air.
    Who calls him Rabbi?
Cart-horse and dogs call him Rabbi,
And he tells them:
The Queen makes every Jew her lover.

And gathering on their green lawns
The people call him Rabbi,
And fill their mouths with good bread
And his happy song.

PRAYER OF MY WILD GRANDFATHER

God, God, God, someone of my family
hated your love with such skill that you sang
to him, your private voice violating
his drum like a lost bee after pollen
in the brain. He gave you his children
opened on a table, and if a ram
ambled in the garden you whispered nothing
about that, nor held his killing hand.

It is no wonder fields and governments
rotted, for soon you gave him all your range,
drove all your love through that sting in his brain.

Nothing can flourish in your absence
except our faith that you are proved through him
who had his mind made mad and honey-combed.

ISAIAH

For G.C.S.

Between the mountains of spices
the cities thrust up pearl domes and filigree spires.
Never before was Jerusalem so beautiful.
    In the sculptured temple how many pilgrims,
lost in the measures of tambourine and lyre,
kneeled before the glory of the ritual?
    Trained in grace the daughters of Zion moved,
not less splendid than the golden statuary,
the bravery of ornaments about their scented feet.
    Government was done in palaces.
Judges, their fortunes found in law,
reclining and cosmopolitan, praised reason.
Commerce like a strong wild garden
    flourished in the street.
The coins were bright, the crest on coins precise,
new ones looked almost wet.

Why did Isaiah rage and cry,
Jerusalem is ruined,
    your cities are burned with fire?

On the fragrant hills of Gilboa
were the shepherds ever calmer,
the sheep fatter, the white wool whiter?
    There were fig trees, cedar, orchards
where men worked in perfume all day long.
New mines as fresh as pomegranates.
    Robbers were gone from the roads,
    the highways were straight.
There were years of wheat against famine.

Enemies? Who has heard of a righteous state
    that has no enemies,
but the young were strong, archers cunning,
    their arrows accurate.

Why then this fool Isaiah,
smelling vaguely of wilderness himself,
why did he shout,
    Your country is desolate?

Now will I sing to my well-beloved
a song of my beloved touching her hair
which is pure metal black
    no rebel prince can change to dross,
of my beloved touching her body
    no false swearer can corrupt,
of my beloved touching her mind
    no faithless counsellor can inflame,
of my beloved touching the mountains of spices
making them beauty instead of burning.

Now plunged in unutterable love
Isaiah wanders, chosen, stumbling
against the sculptured walls which consume
their full age in his embrace and powder
as he goes by. He reels beyond
    the falling dust of spires and domes,
obliterating ritual: the Holy Name, half-spoken,
is lost on the cantor's tongue; their pages barren,
congregations blink, agonized and dumb.
    In the turns of his journey
heavy trees he sleeps under
mature into cinder and crumble:
    whole orchards join the wind

like rising flocks of ravens.

The rocks go back to water, the water to waste.
And while Isaiah gently hums a sound
to make the guilty country uncondemned,
all men, truthfully desolate and lonely,
as though witnessing a miracle,
behold in beauty the faces of one another.

THE GENIUS

For you
I will be a ghetto jew
and dance
and put white stockings
on my twisted limbs
and poison wells
across the town

For you
I will be an apostate jew
and tell the Spanish priest
of the blood vow
in the Talmud
and where the bones
of the child are hid

For you
I will be a banker jew
and bring to ruin
a proud old hunting king
and end his line

For you
I will be a Broadway jew
and cry in theatres
for my mother
and sell bargain goods
beneath the counter

For you
I will be a doctor jew
and search

in all the garbage cans
for foreskins
to sew back again

For you
I will be a Dachau jew
and lie down in lime
with twisted limbs
and bloated pain
no mind can understand

LINES FROM MY GRANDFATHER'S JOURNAL

I am one of those who could tell every word the pin went through. Page after page I could imagine the scar in a thousand crowned letters. . . .

The dancing floor of the pin is bereft of angels. The Christians no longer want to debate. Jews have forgotten the best arguments. If I spelled out the Principles of Faith I would be barking on the moon.

I will never be free from this old tyranny: "I believe with a perfect faith. . . ."

Why make trouble? It is better to stutter than sing. Become like the early Moses: dreamless of Pharaoh. Become like Abram: dreamless of a longer name. Become like a weak Rachel: be comforted, not comfortless. . . .

There was a promise to me from a rainbow, there was a covenant with me after a flood drowned all my friends, inundated every field: the ones we had planted with food and the ones we had left untilled.

Who keeps promises except in business? We were not permitted to own land in Russia. Who wants to own land anywhere? I stare dumbfounded at the trees. Montreal trees, New York trees, Kovno trees. I never wanted to own one. I laugh at the scholars in real estate. . . .

Soldiers in close formation. Paratroops in a white Tel Aviv street. Who dares disdain an answer to the ovens? Any answer.

I did not like to see the young men stunted in the Polish ghetto. Their curved backs were not beautiful. Forgive me, it gives me no pleasure to see them in uniform. I do not thrill to the sight of Jewish battalions.

But there is only one choice between ghettos and battalions, between whips and the weariest patriotic arrogance. . . .

I wanted to keep my body free as when it woke up in Eden. I kept it strong. There are commandments.

Erase from my flesh the marks of my own whip. Heal the razor slashes on my arms and throat. Remove the metal clamps from my fingers. Repair the bones I have crushed in the door.

Do not let me lie down with spiders. Do not let me encourage insects against my eyes. Do not let me make my living nest with worms or apply to my stomach the comb of iron or bind my genitals with cord.

It is strange that even now prayer is my natural language. . . .

Night, my old night. The same in every city, beside every lake. It ambushes a thicket of thrushes. It feeds on the houses and fields. It consumes my journals of poems.

The black, the loss of sun: it will always frighten me. It will always lead me to experiment. My journal is filled with combinations. I adjust prayers like the beads of an abacus. . . .

Thou. Reach into the vineyard of arteries for my heart. Eat the fruit of ignorance and share with me the mist and fragrance of dying.

Thou. Your fist in my chest is heavier than any bereavement, heavier than Eden, heavier than the Torah scroll. . . .

The language in which I was trained: spoken in despair of priestliness.

This is not meant for any pulpit, not for men to chant or tell their children. Not beautiful enough.

But perhaps this can suggest a passion. Perhaps this passion could be brought to clarify, make more radiant, the standing Law.

Let judges secretly despair of justice: their verdicts will be more acute. Let generals secretly despair of triumph; killing will be defamed. Let priests secretly despair of faith: their compassion will be true. It is the tension. . . .

My poems and dictionaries were written at night from my desk or from my bed. Let them cry loudly for life at your hand. Let me be purified by their creation. Challenge me with purity.

O break down these walls with music. Purge from my flesh the need to sleep. Give me eyes for your darkness. Give me legs for your mountains. Let me climb to your face with my argument. If I am unprepared, unclean, lead me first to deserts full of jackals and wolves where I will learn what glory or humility the sand can teach, and from beasts the direction of my evil.

I did not wish to dishonour the scrolls with my logic, or David with my songs. In my work I meant to love you but my voice dissipated somewhere before your infinite regions. And when I gazed toward your eyes all the bristling hills of Judea intervened.

I played with the idea that I was the Messiah. . . .

> I saw a man gouge out his eye,
> hold it in his fist
> until the nursing sky

grew round it like a vast and loving face.
With shafts of light
I saw him mine his wrist
until his blood filled out the rest of space
and settled softly on the world
like morning mist.

Who could resist such fireworks?

I wrestled hard in Galilee.
In the rubbish of pyramids
and strawless bricks
I felled my gentle enemy.
I destroyed his cloak of stars.
It was an insult to our human flesh,
worse than scars.

If we could face his work, submit it to annotation. . . .

You raged before them
like the dreams of their old-time God.
You smashed your body
like tablets of the Law.
You drove them from the temple counters.
Your whip on their loins
was a beginning of trouble.
Your thorns in their hearts
was an end to love.

O come back to our books.
Decorate the Law with human commentary.
Do not invoke a spectacular death.
There is so much to explain—
the miracles obscure your beauty. . . .

Doubting everything that I was made to write. My dictionaries groaning with lies. Driven back to Genesis. Doubting where every word began. What saint had shifted a meaning to illustrate a parable. Even beyond Genesis, until I stood outside my community, like the man who took too many steps on Sabbath. Faced a desolation which was unheroic, unbiblical, no dramatic beasts.

The real deserts are outside of tradition. . . .

The chimneys are smoking. The little wooden synagogues are filled with men. Perhaps they will stumble on my books of interpretation, useful to anyone but me.

The white tablecloths—whiter when you spill the wine. . . .

Desolation means no angels to wrestle. I saw my brothers dance in Poland. Before the final fire I heard them sing. I could not put away my scholarship or my experiments with blasphemy.

(In Prague their Golem slept.)

Desolation means no ravens, no black symbols. The carcass of the rotting dog cannot speak for you. The ovens have no tongue. The flames thud against the stone roofs. I cannot claim that sound.

Desolation means no comparisons. . . .

"Our needs are so manifold, we dare not declare them."

It is painful to recall a past intensity, to estimate your distance from the Belsen heap, to make your peace with numbers. Just to get up each morning is to make a kind of peace.

It is something to have fled several cities. I am glad that I could run, that I could learn twelve languages, that I escaped conscription with a trick, that borders were only stones in an empty road, that I kept my journal.

Let me refuse solutions, refuse to be comforted. . . .

Tonight the sky is luminous. Roads of cloud repeat themselves like the ribs of some vast skeleton.

The easy gulls seem to embody a doomed conception of the sublime as they wheel and disappear into the darkness of the mountain. They leave the heart, they abandon the heart to the Milky Way, that drunkard's glittering line to a physical god. . . .

Sometimes, when the sky is this bright, it seems that if I could only force myself to stare hard at the black hills I could recover the gulls. It seems that nothing is lost that is not forsaken: The rich old treasures still glow in the sand under the tumbled battlement; wrapped in a starry flag a master-God floats through the firmament like a childless kite.

I will never be free from this tyranny.

A tradition composed of the exuviae of visions. I must resist it. It is like the garbage river through a city: beautiful by day and beautiful by night, but always unfit for bathing.

There were beautiful rules: a way to hear thunder, praise a wise man, watch a rainbow, learn of tragedy.

All my family were priests, from Aaron to my father. It was my honour to close the eyes of my famous teacher.

Prayer makes speech a ceremony. To observe this ritual in the absence of arks, altars, a listening sky: this is a rich discipline.

I stare dumbfounded at the trees. I imagine the scar in a thousand crowned letters. Let me never speak casually.

Inscription for the family spice-box:

Make my body
a pomander for worms
and my soul
the fragrance of cloves.

Let the spoiled Sabbath
leave no scent.
Keep my mouth
from foul speech.

Lead your priest
from grave to vineyard.
Lay him down
where air is sweet.

III / Flowers for Hitler

WHAT I'M DOING HERE

I do not know if the world has lied
I have lied
I do not know if the world has conspired against love
I have conspired against love
The atmosphere of torture is no comfort
I have tortured
Even without the mushroom cloud
still I would have hated
Listen
I would have done the same things
even if there were no death
I will not be held like a drunkard
under the cold tap of facts
I refuse the universal alibi

Like an empty telephone booth passed at night
and remembered
like mirrors in a movie palace lobby consulted
only on the way out
like a nymphomaniac who binds a thousand
into strange brotherhood
I wait
for each one of you to confess

THE HEARTH

The day wasn't exactly my own
since I checked
    and found it on a public calendar.
Tripping over many pairs of legs
as I walked down the park
    I also learned my lust
was not so rare a masterpiece.

Buildings actually built
wars planned with blood and fought
men who rose to generals
    deserved an honest thought
as I walked down the park.

I came back quietly to your house
which has a place on a street.
    Not a single other house
disappeared when I came back.
You said some suffering
    had taught me that.

I'm slow to learn I began
to speak of stars and hurricanes.
    Come here little Galileo—
you undressed my vision—
    it's happier and easier by far
or cities wouldn't be so big.

Later you worked over lace
    and I numbered many things
your fingers and all fingers did.

As if to pay me a sweet
    for my ardour on the rug
you wondered in the middle of a stitch:
Now what about those stars and hurricanes?

THE DRAWER'S CONDITION
ON NOVEMBER 28, 1961

Is there anything emptier
than the drawer where
you used to store your opium?
How like a black-eyed susan
blinded into ordinary daisy
is my pretty kitchen drawer!
How like a nose sans nostrils
is my bare wooden drawer!
How like an eggless basket!
How like a pool sans tortoise!
My hand has explored
my drawer like a rat
in an experiment of mazes.
Reader, I may safely say
there's not an emptier drawer
in all of Christendom!

THE SUIT

I am locked in a very expensive suit
old elegant and enduring
Only my hair has been able to get free
but someone has been leaving
their dandruff in it
Now I will tell you
all there is to know about optimism
Each day in hubcap mirror
in soup reflection
in other people's spectacles
I check my hair
for an army of Alpinists
for Indian rope trick masters
for tangled aviators
for dove and albatross
for insect suicides
for abominable snowmen
I check my hair
for aerialists of every kind
Dedicated as an automatic elevator
I comb my hair for possibilities
I stick my neck out
I lean illegally from locomotive windows
and only for the barber
do I wear a hat

INDICTMENT OF THE BLUE HOLE

                          January 28 1962
You must have heard me tonight
I mentioned you 800 times
                          January 28 1962
My abandoned narcotics have
abandoned me
                          January 28 1962
7:30 must have dug its
pikes into your blue wrist
                          January 28 1962
I shoved the transistor up my ear

And putting down
   3 loaves of suicide (?)
   2 razorblade pies
   1 De Quincey hairnet
   ~~5 gasfilled Hampstead bedsitters~~ (sic)
   a collection of oil
   ~~2 eyelash garottes~~ (sic)
   6 lysol eye foods
he said with considerable charm and travail:
Is this all I give?
One lousy reprieve
   at 2 in the morning?
This?
I'd rather have a job.

I WANTED TO BE A DOCTOR

The famous doctor held up Grandma's stomach.
Cancer! Cancer! he cried out.
The theatre was brought low.
None of the internes thought about ambition.

Cancer! They all looked the other way.
They thought Cancer would leap out
and get them. They hated to be near.
This happened in Vilna in the Medical School.

Nobody could sit still.
They might be sitting beside Cancer.
Cancer was present.
Cancer had been let out of its bottle.

I was looking in the skylight.
I wanted to be a doctor.
All the internes ran outside.
The famous doctor held on to the stomach.

He was alone with Cancer.
Cancer! Cancer! Cancer!
He didn't care who heard or didn't hear.
It was his 87th Cancer.

ON HEARING A NAME
LONG UNSPOKEN

Listen to the stories
men tell of last year
that sound of other places
though they happened here

Listen to a name
so private it can burn
hear it said aloud
and learn and learn

History is a needle
for putting men asleep
anointed with the poison
of all they want to keep

Now a name that saved you
has a foreign taste
claims a foreign body
froze in last year's waste

And what is living lingers
while monuments are built
then yields its final whisper
to letters raised in gilt

But cries of stifled ripeness
whip me to my knees
I am with the falling snow
falling in the seas

I am with the hunters
hungry and shrewd

and I am with the hunted
quick and soft and nude

I am with the houses
that wash away in rain
and leave no teeth of pillars
to rake them up again

Let men numb names
scratch winds that blow
listen to the stories
but what you know you know

And knowing is enough
for mountains such as these
where nothing long remains
houses walls or trees

STYLE

I don't believe the radio stations
of Russia and America
but I like the music and I like
the solemn European voices announcing jazz
I don't believe opium or money
though they're hard to get
and punished with long sentences
I don't believe love
in the midst of my slavery I
do not believe
I am a man sitting in a house
on a treeless Argolic island
I will forget the grass of my mother's lawn
I know I will
I will forget the old telephone number
Fitzroy seven eight two oh
I will forget my style
I will have no style
I hear a thousand miles of hungry static
and the old clear water eating rocks
I hear the bells of mules eating
I hear the flowers eating the night
under their folds
Now a rooster with a razor
plants the haemophilia gash across
the soft black sky
and now I know for certain
I will forget my style
Perhaps a mind will open in this world
perhaps a heart will catch rain
Nothing will heal and nothing will freeze
but perhaps a heart will catch rain

America will have no style
Russia will have no style
It is happening in the twenty-eighth year
of my attention
I don't know what will become
of the mules with their lady eyes
or the old clear water
or the giant rooster
The early morning greedy radio eats
the governments one by one the languages
the poppy fields one by one
Beyond the numbered band
a silence develops for every style
for the style I laboured on
an external silence like the space
between insects in a swarm
electric unremembering
and it is aimed at us
(I am sleepy and frightened)
it makes toward me brothers

GOEBBELS ABANDONS HIS NOVEL
AND JOINS THE PARTY

His last love poem
        broke in the harbour
where swearing blondes
loaded scrap
        into rusted submarines.
Out in the sun
he was surprised
        to find himself lustless
as a wheel.
More simple than money
he sat in some spilled salt
and wondered if he would find again
the scars of lampposts
ulcers of wrought-iron fence.
He remembered perfectly
how he sprung
        his father's heart attack
and left his mother
in a pit
memory white from loss of guilt.
Precision in the sun
the elevators
        the pieces of iron
broke whatever thous
        his pain had left
like a whistle breaks
a gang of sweating men.
Ready to join the world
yes yes ready to marry
convinced pain a matter of choice
a Doctor of Reason

he began to count the ships
decorate the men.
Will dreams threaten
    this discipline
will favourite hair favourite thighs
last life's sweepstake winners
drive him to adventurous cafés?
Ah my darling pupils
do you think there exists a hand
so bestial in beauty so ruthless
that can switch off
his religious electric Exlax light?

HITLER THE BRAIN-MOLE

Hitler the brain-mole looks out of my eyes
Goering boils ingots of gold in my bowels
My Adam's Apple bulges with the whole head of Goebbels
No use to tell a man he's a Jew
I'm making a lampshade out of your kiss
Confess! confess!
    is what you demand
although you believe you're giving me everything

IT USES US!

Come upon this heap
exposed to camera leer:
would you snatch a skull
for midnight wine, my dear?

Can you wear a cape
claim these burned for you
or is this death unusable
alien and new?

In our leaders' faces
(albeit they deplore
the past) can you read how
they love Freedom more?

In my own mirror
their eyes beam at me:
my face is theirs, my eyes
burnt and free.

Now you and I are mounted
on this heap, my dear:
from this height we thrill
as boundaries disappear.

Kiss me with your teeth.

All things can be done
whisper museum ovens of
a war that Freedom won.

MY TEACHER IS DYING

Martha they say you are gentle
No doubt you labour at it
Why is it I see you
leaping into unmade beds
strangling the telephone
Why is it I see you
hiding your dirty nylons
in the fireplace
Martha talk to me
My teacher is dying
His laugh is already dead
that put cartilage
between the bony facts
Now they rattle loud
Martha talk to me
Mountain Street is dying
Apartment fifteen is dying
Apartment seven and eight are dying
All the rent is dying
Martha talk to me
I wanted all the dancers' bodies
to inhabit like his old classroom
where everything that happened
was tender and important
Martha talk to me
Toss out the fake Jap silence
Scream in my kitchen
logarithms laundry lists anything
Talk to me
My radio is falling to pieces
My betrayals are so fresh
they still come with explanations

Martha talk to me
What sordid parable
do you teach by sleeping
Talk to me
for my teacher is dying
The cars are parked
on both sides of the street
some facing north
some facing south
I draw no conclusions
Martha talk to me
I could burn my desk
when I think how perfect we are
you asleep me finishing
the last of the Saint Emilion
Talk to me gentle Martha
dreaming of percussions massacres
hair pinned to the ceiling
I'll keep your secret
Let's tell the milkman
we have decided
to marry our rooms

FOR MY OLD LAYTON

His pain, unowned, he left
in paragraphs of love, hidden,
like a cat leaves shit
under stones, and he crept out in day,
clean, arrogant, swift, prepared
to hunt or sleep or starve.

The town saluted him with garbage
which he interpreted as praise
for his muscular grace. Orange peels,
cans, discarded guts rained like ticker-tape.
For a while he ruined their nights
by throwing his shadow in moon-full windows
as he spied on the peace of gentle folk.

Once he envied them. Now with a happy
screech he bounded from monument to monument
in their most consecrated plots, drunk
to know how close he lived to the breathless
in the ground, drunk to feel how much he loved
the snoring mates, the old, the children of the town.

Until at last, like Timon, tired
of human smell, resenting even
his own shoe-steps in the wilderness,
he chased animals, wore live snakes, weeds
for bracelets. When the sea
pulled back the tide like a blanket
he slept on stone cribs, heavy,
dreamless, the salt-bright atmosphere
like an automatic laboratory
building crystals in his hair.

FINALLY I CALLED

Finally I called the people I didn't want to hear from
After the third ring I said
I'll let it ring five more times then what will I do
The telephone is a fine instrument
but I never learned to work it very well
Five more rings and I'll put the receiver down
I know where it goes I know that much
The telephone was black with silver rims
The booth was cozier than the drugstore
There were a lot of creams and scissors and tubes
I needed for my body
I was interested in many coughdrops
I believe the drugstore keeper hated
his telephone and people like me
who ask for change so politely
I decided to keep to the same street
and go into the fourth drugstore
and call them again

THE ONLY TOURIST IN HAVANA
TURNS HIS THOUGHTS HOMEWARD

Come, my brothers,
let us govern Canada,
let us find our serious heads,
let us dump asbestos on the White House,
let us make the French talk English,
    not only here but everywhere,
let us torture the Senate individually
    until they confess,
let us purge the New Party,
let us encourage the dark races
    so they'll be lenient
    when they take over,
let us make the CBC talk English,
let us all lean in one direction
    and float down
    to the coast of Florida,
let us have tourism,
let us flirt with the enemy,
let us smelt pig-iron in our back yards,
let us sell snow
    to under-developed nations,
(Is it true one of our national leaders
    was a Roman Catholic?)
let us terrorize Alaska,
let us unite
    Church and State,
let us not take it lying down,
let us have two Governor Generals
    at the same time,
let us have another official language,
let us determine what it will be,

let us give a Canada Council Fellowship
   to the most original suggestion,
let us teach sex in the home
   to parents,
let us threaten to join the U.S.A.
   and pull out at the last moment,
my brothers, come,
our serious heads are waiting for us somewhere
   like Gladstone bags abandoned
   after a *coup d'état,*
let us put them on very quickly,
let us maintain a stony silence
   on the St. Lawrence Seaway.

Havana
April 1961

This could be my little
　　book about love
　　　if I wrote it—
but my good demon said:
　"Lay off documents!"
Everybody was watching me
　　burn my books—
　I swung my liberty torch
　happy as a gestapo brute;
　the only thing I wanted to save
　　　　was a scar
　　　　a burn or two—
　　but my good demon said:
　　"Lay off documents!
　　The fire's not important!"
The pile was safely blazing.
I went home to take a bath.
I phoned my grandmother.
She is suffering from arthritis.
"Keep well," I said, "don't mind the pain."
　　　"You neither," she said.
Hours later I wondered
　　　did she mean
　　don't mind *my* pain
　　or don't mind *her* pain?
　Whereupon my good demon said:
　　"Is that all you can do?"
　　　Well was it?
　　Was it all I could do?
　　There was the old lady
　　eating alone, thinking about
　　　Prince Albert, Flanders Field,

my personal fire

Kishenev, her fingers too sore
        for TV knobs;
      but how could I get there?
   The books were gone
      my address lists—
My good demon said again:
"Lay off documents!
   You know how to get there!"
   And suddenly I did!
I remembered it from memory!
      I found her
poring over the royal family tree,
        "Grandma,"
      I almost said,
   "you've got it upside down—"
   "Take a look," she said,
   "it only goes to George V."
      "That's far enough
        you sweet old blood!"
      "You're right!" she sang
        and burned the
      London Illustrated Souvenir
I did not understand
        the day it was
        till I looked outside
        and saw a fire in every
        window on the street
      and crowds of humans
        crazy to talk
and cats and dogs and birds
      smiling at each other!

fires in every window

animals in love

ALEXANDER TROCCHI, PUBLIC JUNKIE, PRIEZ POUR NOUS

Who is purer
    more simple than you?
Priests play poker with the burghers,
police in underwear
    leave Crime at the office,
our poets work bankers' hours
retire to wives and fame-reports.

The spike flashes in your blood
permanent as a silver lighthouse.

I'm apt to loaf
    in a coma of newspapers,
avoid the second-hand bodies
which cry to be catalogued.
I dream I'm
    a divine right Prime Minister,
I abandon plans for bloodshed in Canada.
I accept an O.B.E.

Under hard lights
with doctors' instruments
    you are at work
in the bathrooms of the city,
changing The Law.

I tend to get distracted
    by hydrogen bombs,
by Uncle's disapproval
    of my treachery
to the men's clothing industry.

I find myself
  believing public clocks,
taking advice
from the Dachau generation.

The spike hunts
constant as a compass.
  You smile like a Navajo
discovering American oil
on his official slum wilderness,
a surprise every half hour.

I'm afraid I sometimes forget
my lady's pretty little blond package
is an amateur time-bomb
set to fizzle in my middle-age.
  I forget the Ice Cap, the pea-minds,
the heaps of expensive teeth.

You don a false nose
line up twice for the Demerol dole;
you step out of a tourist group
shoot yourself on the steps of the White House,
you try to shoot the big arms
  of the Lincoln Memorial;
through a flaw in their lead houses
you spy on scientists,
  stumble on a cure for scabies;
you drop pamphlets from a stolen jet:
"The Truth about Junk";
you pirate a national TV commercial
shove your face against
  the window of the living-room
insist that healthy skin is grey.

A little blood in the sink
Red cog-wheels
    shaken from your arm
punctures inflamed
like a roadmap showing cities
over 10,000 pop.

Your arms tell me
you have been reaching into the coke machine
for strawberries,
you have been humping the thorny crucifix
you have been piloting Mickey Mouse balloons
through the briar patch,
you have been digging for grins in the tooth-pile.

Bonnie Queen Alex Eludes Montreal Hounds
Famous Local Love Scribe Implicated

Your purity drives me to work.
I must get back to lust and microscopes,
experiments in embalming,
resume the census of my address book.

You leave behind you a fanatic
to answer RCMP questions.

THREE GOOD NIGHTS

Out of some simple part of me
which I cannot use up
    I took a blessing for the flowers
tightening in the night
like fists of jealous love
    like knots
no one can undo without destroying
    The new morning gathered me
in blue mist
    like dust under a wedding gown
Then I followed the day
like a cloud of heavy sheep
    after the judas
up a blood-ringed ramp
into the terror of every black building

Ten years sealed journeys unearned dreams
Laughter meant to tempt me into old age
    spilled for friends stars unknown flesh mules sea
Instant knowledge of bodies material and spirit
    which slowly learned would have made death smile
Stories turning into theories
    which begged only for the telling and retelling
Girls sailing over the blooms of my mouth
    with a muscular triangular kiss
    ordinary mouth to secret mouth
Nevertheless my homage sticky flowers
    rabbis green and red serving the sun like platters
In the end you offered me the dogma you taught
    me to disdain and I good pupil disdained it
I fell under the diagrammed fields like the fragment
    of a perfect statue layers of cities build upon

I saw you powerful I saw you happy
    that I could not live only for harvesting
that I was a true citizen of the slow earth

Light and Splendour
in the sleeping orchards
entering the trees
like a silent movie wedding procession
entering the arches of branches
for the sake of love only
From a hill I watched
the apple blossoms breathe
the silver out of the night
like fish eating the spheres
of air out of the river
So the illumined night fed
the sleeping orchards
entering the vaults of branches
like a holy procession
Long live the Power of Eyes
Long live the invisible steps
men can read on a mountain
Long live the unknown machine
or heart
which by will or accident
pours with victor's grace
endlessly perfect weather
on the perfect creatures
the world grows

Montreal
July 1964

ON THE SICKNESS OF MY LOVE

Poems! break out!
break my head!
What good's a skull?
Help! help!
I need you!

She is getting old.
Her body tells her everything.
She has put aside cosmetics.
She is a prison of truth.

Make her get up!
dance the seven veils!
Poems! silence her body!
Make her friend of mirrors!

Do I have to put on my cape?
wander like the moon
over skies & skies of flesh
to depart again in the morning?

Can't I pretend
she grows prettier?
be a convict?
Can't my power fool me?
Can't I live in poems?

Hurry up! poems! lies!
Damn your weak music!
You've let arthritis in!
You're no poem
you're a visa.

FOR MARIANNE

It's so simple
to wake up beside your ears
and count the pearls
with my two heads

It takes me back to blackboards
and I'm running with Jane
and seeing the dog run

It makes it so easy
to govern this country
I've already thought up the laws
I'll work hard all day
in Parliament

Then let's go to bed
right after supper
Let's sleep and wake up
all night

THE FAILURE OF A SECULAR LIFE

The pain-monger came home
from a hard day's torture.

He came home with his tongs.
He put down his black bag.

His wife hit him with an open nerve
and a cry the trade never heard.

He watched her real-life Dachau,
knew his career was ruined.

Was there anything else to do?
He sold his bag and tongs,

went to pieces. A man's got to be able
to bring his wife something.

MY MENTORS

My rabbi has a silver buddha,
my priest has a jade talisman.
My doctor sees a marvellous omen
in our prolonged Indian summer.

My rabbi, my priest stole their trinkets
from shelves in the holy of holies.
The trinkets cannot be eaten.
They wonder what to do with them.

My doctor is happy as a pig
although he is dying of exposure.
He has finished his big book
on the phallus as a phallic symbol.

My zen master is a grand old fool.
I caught him worshipping me yesterday,
so I made him stand in a foul corner
with my rabbi, my priest, and my doctor.

HEIRLOOM

The torture scene developed under a glass bell
such as might protect an expensive clock.
I almost expected a chime to sound
as the tongs were applied
and the body jerked and fainted calm.
All the people were tiny and rosy-cheeked
and if I could have heard a cry of triumph or pain
it would have been tiny as the mouth that made it
or one single note of a music box.
The drama bell was mounted
like a gigantic baroque pearl
on a wedding ring or brooch or locket.

    I know you feel naked, little darling.
I know you hate living in the country
and can't wait until the shiny magazines
come every week and every month.
Look through your grandmother's house again.
There is an heirloom somewhere.

Evidently they need a lot of blood for these tests. I let them take all they wanted. The hospital was cool and its atmosphere of order encouraged me to persist in my own projects.

I always wanted to set fire to your houses. I've been in them. Through the front doors and the back. I'd like to see them burn slowly so I could visit many and peek in the falling windows. I'd like to see what happens to those white carpets you pretended to be so careless about. I'd like to see a white telephone melting.

We don't want to trap too many inside because the streets have got to be packed with your poor bodies screaming back and forth. I'll be comforting. Oh dear, pyjama flannel seared right on to the flesh. Let me pull it off.

It seems to me they took too much blood. Probably selling it on the side. The little man's white frock was smeared with blood. Little men like that keep company with blood. See them in *abattoirs* and assisting in human experiments.

—When did you last expose yourself?

—Sunday morning for a big crowd in the lobby of the Queen Elizabeth.

—Funny. You know what I mean.

—Expose myself to what?

—A woman.

—Ah.

I narrowed my eyes and whispered in his yellow ear.

—You better bring her in too.

—And it's still free?

Of course it was still free. Not counting the extra blood they stole. Prevent my disease from capturing the entire city. Help this man. Give him all possible Judeo-Christian help.

Fire would be best. I admit that. Tie firebrands between

118 |

the foxes and chase them through your little gardens. A rosy sky would improve the view from anywhere. It would be a mercy. Oh, to see the roofs devoured and the beautiful old level of land rising again.

The factory where I work isn't far from the hospital. Same architect as a matter of fact and the similarities don't end there. It's easier to get away with lying down in the hospital. However we have our comforts in the factory.

The foreman winked at me when I went back to my machine. He loved his abundant nature. Me new at the job and he'd actually given me time off. I really enjoy the generosity of slaves. He came over to inspect my work.

—But this won't do at all.

—No?

—The union said you were an experienced operator.

—I am. I am.

—This is no seam.

—Now that you mention it.

—Look here.

He took a fresh trouser and pushed in beside me on the bench. He was anxious to demonstrate the only skill he owned. He arranged the pieces under the needle. When he was halfway down the leg and doing very nicely I brought my foot down on the pedal beside his. The unexpected acceleration sucked his fingers under the needle.

Another comfort is the Stock Room.

It is large and dark and filled with bundles and rolls of material.

—But shouldn't you be working?

—No, Mary, I shouldn't.

—Won't Sam miss you?

—You see he's in the hospital. Accident.

Mary runs the Cafeteria and the Boss exposes himself to her regularly. This guarantees her the concession.

I feel the disease raging in my blood. I expect my saliva to be discoloured.

—Yes, Mary, real cashmere. Three hundred dollar suits.

The Boss has a wife to whom he must expose himself every once in a while. She has her milkmen. The city is orderly. There are white bottles standing in front of a million doors. And there are Conventions. Multitudes of bosses sharing the pleasures of exposure.

I shall go mad. They'll find me at the top of Mount Royal impersonating Genghis Khan. Seized with laughter and pus.

—Very soft, Mary. That's what they pay for.

Fire would be best. Flames. Bright windows. Two cars exploding in each garage. But could I ever manage it. This way is slower. More heroic in a way. Less dramatic of course. But I have an imagination.

HYDRA 1963

The stony path coiled around me
and bound me to the night.
A boat hunted the edge of the sea
under a hissing light.

Something soft involved a net
and bled around a spear.
The blunt death, the cumulus jet—
I spoke to you, I thought you near!

Or was the night so black
that something died alone?
A man with a glistening back
beat the food against a stone.

ALL THERE IS TO KNOW
ABOUT ADOLPH EICHMANN

EYES: .... Medium
HAIR: .... Medium
WEIGHT: .... Medium
HEIGHT: .... Medium
DISTINGUISHING FEATURES: .... None
NUMBER OF FINGERS: .... Ten
NUMBER OF TOES: .... Ten
INTELLIGENCE: .... Medium

What did you expect?

Talons?

Oversize incisors?

Green saliva?

Madness?

When he learned that his father had the oven contract, that the smoke above the city, the clouds as warm as skin, were his father's manufacture, he was freed from love, his emptiness was legalized.

Hygienic as a whip his heart drove out the alibis of devotion, free as a storm-severed bridge, useless and pure as drowned alarm clocks, he breathed deeply, gratefully in the polluted atmosphere, and he announced: My father had the oven contract, he loved my mother and built her houses in the countryside.

When he learned his father had the oven contract he climbed a hillock of eyeglasses, he stood on a drift of hair, he hated with great abandon the king cripples and their mothers, the husbands and wives, the familiar sleep, the decent burdens.

Dancing down Ste Catherine Street he performed great surgery on a hotel of sleepers. The windows leaked like a broken meat freezer. His hatred blazed white on the salted driveways. He missed nobody but he was happy he'd taken one hunded and fifty women in moonlight back in ancient history.

He was drunk at last, drunk at last, after years of threading history's crushing daisy-chain with beauty after beauty. His father had raised the thigh-shaped clouds which smelled of salesmen, gipsies and violinists. With the certainty and genital pleasure of revelation he knew, he could not doubt, his father was the one who had the oven contract.

Drunk at last, he hugged himself, his stomach clean, cold and drunk, the sky clean but only for him, free to shiver, free to hate, free to begin.

FOR E.J.P.

I once believed a single line
    in a Chinese poem could change
        forever how blossoms fell
and that the moon itself climbed on
    the grief of concise weeping men
        to journey over cups of wine
I thought invasions were begun for crows
    to pick at a skeleton
        dynasties sown and spent
to serve the language of a fine lament
    I thought governors ended their lives
        as sweetly drunken monks
telling time by rain and candles
    instructed by an insect's pilgrimage
        across the page—all this
so one might send an exile's perfect letter
to an ancient home-town friend

I chose a lonely country
    broke from love
        scorned the fraternity of war
I polished my tongue against the pumice moon
    floated my soul in cherry wine
        a perfumed barge for Lords of Memory
to languish on to drink to whisper out
    their store of strength
        as if beyond the mist along the shore
their girls their power still obeyed
    like clocks wound for a thousand years
I waited until my tongue was sore

Brown petals wind like fire around my poems
    I aimed them at the stars but
        like rainbows they were bent
before they sawed the world in half
    Who can trace the canyoned paths
        cattle have carved out of time
wandering from meadowlands to feasts
    Layer after layer of autumn leaves
        are swept away
Something forgets us perfectly

A MIGRATING DIALOGUE

He was wearing a black moustache and leather hair.
We talked about the gipsies.

Don't bite your nails, I told him.
Don't eat carpets.
Be careful of the rabbits.
Be cute.
Don't stay up all night watching
parades on the Very Very Very Late Show.
Don't ka-ka in your uniform.

And what about all the good generals,
the fine old aristocratic fighting men,
the brave Junkers, the brave Rommels,
the brave von Silverhaired Ambassadors
who resigned in '41?

Wipe that smirk off your face.
Captain Marvel signed the whip contract.
Joe Palooka manufactured whips.
Li'l Abner packed the whips in cases.
The Katzenjammer Kids thought up experiments.
Mere cogs.

Peekaboo Miss Human Soap.
It never happened.
O castles on the Rhine.
O blond SS.
Don't believe everything you see in museums.

I said WIPE THAT SMIRK including
the mouth-foam of superior disgust.
I don't like the way you go to work every morning.
How come the buses still run?
How come they're still making movies?

I believe with a perfect faith in the Second World War.
I am convinced that it happened.
I am not so sure about the First World War.
The Spanish Civil War—maybe.
I believe in gold teeth.
I believe in Churchill.
Don't tell me we dropped fire into cribs.
I think you are exaggerating.
The Treaty of Westphalia has faded like a lipstick
smudge on the Blarney Stone.
Napoleon was a sexy brute.
Hiroshima was Made in Japan out of paper.
I think we should let sleeping ashes lie.
I believe with a perfect faith in all the history
I remember, but it's getting harder and harder
to remember much history.

There is sad confetti sprinkling
from the windows of departing trains.
I let them go. I cannot remember them.
They hoot mournfully out of my daily life.
I forget the big numbers,
I forget what they mean.
I apologize to the special photogravure section
of a 1945 newspaper which began my education.
I apologize left and right.
I apologize in advance to all the folks
in this fine wide audience for my tasteless closing remarks.

Braun, Raubal and him
Hitler and his ladies
(I have some experience in these matters),
these three humans,
I can't get their nude and loving bodies out of my mind.

THE BUS

I was the last passenger of the day,
I was alone on the bus,
I was glad they were spending all that money
just getting me up Eighth Avenue.
Driver! I shouted, it's you and me tonight,
let's run away from this big city
to a smaller city more suitable to the heart,
let's drive past the swimming pools of Miami Beach,
you in the driver's seat, me several seats back,
but in the racial cities we'll change places
so as to show how well you've done up North,
and let us find ourselves some tiny American fishing village
in unknown Florida
and park right at the edge of the sand,
a huge bus pointing out,
metallic, painted, solitary,
with New York plates.

THE REST IS DROSS

We meet at a hotel
with many quarters for the radio
surprised that we've survived as lovers
not each other's
but lovers still
with outrageous hope and habits in the craft
which embarrass us slightly
as we let them be known
the special caress the perfect inflammatory word
the starvation we do not tell about
We do what only lovers can
  make a gift out of necessity
Looking at our clothes
folded over the chair
I see we no longer follow fashion
and we own our own skins
God I'm happy we've forgotten nothing
and can love each other
for years in the world

I ask you where you want to go
you say nowhere
    but your eyes make a wish
An absent chiropractor
you stroke my wrist
    I'm almost fooled into
greasy circular snores
when I notice your eyes
    sounding the wall for
dynamite points
like a doctor at work on a TB chest
    Nowhere you say again in a kiss
go to sleep
First tell me your wish
    Your lashes startle on my skin
like a seismograph
An airliner's perishing drone
    pulls the wall off our room
like an old Band-aid
The winter comes in
    and the eyes I don't keep
tie themselves to a journey
like wedding tin cans

Ways Mills
November 1963

PROPAGANDA

The coherent statement was made
by father, the gent with spats to
keep his shoes secret. It had to
do with the nature of religion and
the progress of lust in the twentieth
century. I myself have several
statements of a competitive
coherence which I intend to spread
around at no little expense. I
love the eternal moment, for
instance. My father used to remark,
doffing his miniature medals, that
there is a time that is ripe for
everything. A little extravagant,
Dad, I guess, judging by values.
Oh well, he'd say, and the whole
world might have been the address.

Several faiths
bid him leap—
opium and Hitler
let him sleep.

A Negress with
an appetite
helped him think
he wasn't white.

Opium and Hitler
made him sure
the world was glass.
There was no cure

for matter
disarmed as this:
the state rose on
a festered kiss.

Once a dream
nailed on the sky
a summer sun
while it was high.

He wanted a
blindfold of skin,
he wanted the
afternoon to begin.

One law broken—
nothing held.

The world was wax,
his to mould.

No! He fumbled
for his history dose.
The sun came loose,
his woman close.

Lost in a darkness
their bodies would reach,
the Leader started
a racial speech.

FOR ANYONE DRESSED IN MARBLE

The miracle we all are waiting for
is waiting till the Parthenon falls down
and House of Birthdays is a house no more
and fathers are unpoisoned by renown.
The medals and the records of abuse
can't help us on our pilgrimage to lust,
but like whips certain perverts never use,
compel our flesh in paralysing trust.
    I see an orphan, lawless and serene,
standing in a corner of the sky,
body something like bodies that have been,
but not the scar of naming in his eye.
Bred close to the ovens, he's burnt inside.
Light, wind, cold, dark—they use him like a bride.

FOLK

flowers for hitler the summer yawned
flowers all over my new grass
and here is a little village
they are painting it for a holiday
here is a little church
here is a school
here are some doggies making love
the flags are bright as laundry
flowers for hitler the summer yawned

I HAD IT FOR A MOMENT

I had it for a moment
I knew why I must thank you
    I saw powerful governing men in black suits
I saw them undressed
in the arms of young mistresses
the men more naked than the naked women
the men crying quietly
    No that is not it
I'm losing why I must thank you
which means I'm left with pure longing
    How old are you
Do you like your thighs
I had it for a moment
I had a reason for letting the picture
of your mouth destroy my conversation
    Something on the radio
the end of a Mexican song
I saw the musicians getting paid
they are not even surprised
they knew it was only a job
    Now I've lost it completely
A lot of people think you are beautiful
How do I feel about that
I have no feeling about that
    I had a wonderful reason for not merely
courting you
It was tied up with the newspapers
    I saw secret arrangements in high offices
I saw men who loved their worldliness
even though they had looked through
big electric telescopes
they still thought their worldliness was serious

not just a hobby a taste a harmless affectation
    they thought the cosmos listened
I was suddenly fearful
one of their obscure regulations
could separate us
    I was ready to beg for mercy
Now I'm getting into humiliation
I've lost why I began this
I wanted to talk about your eyes
I know nothing about your eyes
and you've noticed how little I know
I want you somewhere safe
far from high offices
    I'll study you later
So many people want to cry quietly beside you

July 4, 1963

INDEPENDENCE

Tonight I will live with my new white skin
which I found under a millennium of pith clothing
None of the walls jump when I call them
Trees smirked *you're one of us now*
when I strode through the wheat in my polished boots
Out of control awake and newly naked
I lie back in the luxury of my colour
Somebody is marching for me at me to me
Somebody has a flag I did not invent
I think the Aztecs have not been sleeping
Magic moves from hand to hand like money
I thought we were the bank the end of the line
New York City was just a counter
the crumpled bill passed across
I thought that heroes meant us
I have been reading too much history
and writing too many history books
Magic moves from hand to hand and I'm broke
Someone stops the sleepwalker in the middle of the opera
and pries open his fist finger by finger
and kisses him goodbye
I think the Aztecs have not been sleeping
no matter what I taught the children
I think no one has ever slept but he
who gathers the past into stories
Magic moves from hand to hand
Somebody is smiling in one of our costumes
Somebody is stepping out of a costume
I think that is what invisible means

July 4, 1963

THE HOUSE

Two hours off the branch and burnt
the petals of the gardenia curl and deepen
in the yellow-brown of waste
    Your body wandered close
    I didn't raise my hand to reach
the distance was so familiar
Our house is happy with its old furniture
the black Venetian bed stands on gold claws
guarding the window
    Don't take the window away
    and leave a hole in the stark mountains
The clothesline and the grey clothespins
would make you think we're going to be together always
    Last night I dreamed
    you were Buddha's wife
and I was a historian watching you sleep
What vanity
    A girl told me something beautiful
    Very early in the morning
she saw an orange-painted wooden boat
come into port over the smooth sea
The cargo was hay
The boat rode low under the weight
She couldn't see the sailors
but on top of all the hay sat a monk
Because of the sun behind he seemed
to be sitting in a fire
like that famous photograph
    I forgot to tell you the story
    She surprised me by telling it
and I wanted her for ten minutes
I really enjoyed the gardenia from Sophia's courtyard

You put it on my table two hours ago
        and I can smell it everywhere in the house
Darling I attach nothing to it

July 4, 1963

THE LISTS

Strafed by the Milky Way
vaccinated by a snarl of clouds
lobotomized by the bore of the moon
he fell in a heap
some woman's smell
smeared across his face
a plan for Social Welfare
rusting in a trouser cuff
        From five to seven
tall trees doctored him
mist roamed on guard
        Then it began again
the sun stuck a gun in his mouth
the wind started to skin him
Give up the Plan give up the Plan
echoing among its scissors
        The women who elected him
performed erotic calisthenics
above the stock-reports
of every hero's fame
        Out of the corner of his stuffed eye
etched in minor metal
under his letter of the alphabet
he clearly saw his tiny name
        Then a museum slid under
his remains like a shovel

ORDER

In many movies I came upon an idol
I would not touch, whose forehead jewel
was safe, or if stolen—mourned.
Truly, I wanted the lost forbidden city
to be the labyrinth for wise technicolor
birds, and every human riddle
the love-fed champion pursued
I knew was bad disguise for greed.
I was with the snake who made his nest
in the voluptuous treasure, I dropped
with the spider to threaten the trail-bruised
white skin of the girl who was searching
for her brother, I balanced on the limb
with the leopard who had to be content
with Negroes and double-crossers
and never tasted but a slash of hero flesh.
Even after double-pay I deserted
with the bearers, believing every rumour
the wind brought from the mountain pass.
The old sorceress, the spilled wine,
the black cards convinced me:
the timeless laws must not be broken.
When the lovers got away with the loot
of new-valued life or love, or bought
themselves a share in time by letting
the avalanche seal away for ever
the gold goblets and platters, I knew
a million ways the jungle might have been
meaner and smarter. As the red sun

came down on their embrace I shouted
from my velvet seat, Get them, get them,
to all the animals drugged with anarchy and happiness.

August 6, 1963

DESTINY

I want your warm body to disappear
politely and leave me alone in the bath
because I want to consider my destiny.
Destiny! why do you find me in this bathtub,
idle, alone, unwashed, without even
the intention of washing except at the last moment?
Why don't you find me at the top of a telephone pole,
repairing the lines from city to city?
Why don't you find me riding a horse through Cuba,
a giant of a man with a red machete?
Why don't you find me explaining machines
to underprivileged pupils, negroid Spaniards,
happy it is not a course in creative writing?
Come back here, little warm body,
it's time for another day.
Destiny has fled and I settle for you
who found me staring at you in a store
one afternoon four years ago
and slept with me every night since.
How do you find my sailor eyes after all this time?
Am I what you expected?
Are we together too much?
Did Destiny shy at the double Turkish towel,
our knowledge of each other's skin,
our love which is a proverb on the block,
our agreement that in matters spiritual
I should be the Man of Destiny
and you should be the Woman of the House?

QUEEN VICTORIA AND ME

Queen Victoria
my father and all his tobacco loved you
I love you too in all your forms
the slim unlovely virgin anyone would lay
the white figure floating among German beards
the mean governess of the huge pink maps
the solitary mourner of a prince
Queen Victoria
I am cold and rainy
I am dirty as a glass roof in a train station
I feel like an empty cast-iron exhibition
I want ornaments on everything
because my love she gone with other boys
Queen Victoria
do you have a punishment under the white lace
will you be short with her
and make her read little Bibles
will you spank her with a mechanical corset
I want her pure as power
I want her skin slightly musty with petticoats
will you wash the easy bidets out of her head
Queen Victoria
I'm not much nourished by modern love
Will you come into my life
with your sorrow and your black carriages
and your perfect memory
Queen Victoria
The 20th century belongs to you and me
Let us be two severe giants
(not less lonely for our partnership)
who discolour test tubes in the halls of science

who turn up unwelcome at every World's Fair
heavy with proverb and correction
confusing the star-dazed tourists
with our incomparable sense of loss

THE NEW STEP

A Ballet-Drama in One Act

CHARACTERS:

MARY and DIANE, two working girls who room together. MARY is very plain, plump, clumsy: ugly, if one is inclined to the word. She is the typical victim of beauty courses and glamour magazines. Her life is a search for, a belief in the technique, the elixir, the method, the secret, the hint that will transform and render her forever lovely. DIANE is a natural beauty, tall, fresh and graceful, one of the blessed. She moves to a kind of innocent sexual music, incapable of any gesture which could intrude on this high animal grace. To watch her pull on her nylons is all one needs of ballet or art.

HARRY is the man DIANE loves. He has the proportions we associate with Greek statuary. Clean, tall, openly handsome, athletic. He glitters with health, decency, and mindlessness.

THE COLLECTOR is a woman over thirty, grotesquely obese, a great heap, deformed, barely mobile. She possesses a commanding will and combines the fascination of the tyrant and the freak. Her jolliness asks for no charity. All her movements represent the triumph of a rather sinister spiritual energy over an intolerable mass of flesh.

SCENE:

It is eight o'clock of a Saturday night. All the action takes place in the girls' small apartment which need be furnished with no more than a dressing-mirror, wardrobe, recordplayer, easy chair, and a front door. We have the impression, as we do from the dwelling places of most bachelor girls, of an arrangement they want to keep comfortable but temporary.

DIANE is dressed in bra and panties, preparing herself for an evening with HARRY. MARY follows her about the room, lost in envy and awe, handing DIANE the necessary lipstick or brush, doing up a button or fastening a necklace. MARY is the dull but orthodox assistant to DIANE's mysterious ritual of beauty.

MARY: What is it like?

DIANE: What like?

MARY: You know.

DIANE: No.

MARY: To be like you.

DIANE: Such as?

MARY: Beautiful.

(*Pause. During these pauses* DIANE *continues her toilet as does* MARY *her attendance.*)

DIANE: Everybody can be beautiful.

MARY: You can say that.

DIANE: Love makes people beautiful.

MARY: You can say that.

DIANE: A woman in love is beautiful.

(*Pause.*)

MARY: Look at me.

DIANE: I've got to hurry.

MARY: Harry always waits.

DIANE: He said he's got something on his mind.

MARY: You've got the luck.

(*Pause.*)

MARY: Look at me a second.

DIANE: All right.

(MARY *performs an aggressive curtsy.*)

MARY: Give me some advice.

DIANE: Everybody has their points.

MARY: What are my points?

DIANE: What are your points?

MARY: Name my points.

(MARY *stands there belligerently. She lifts up her skirt. She rolls up her sleeves. She tucks her sweater in tight.*)

DIANE: I've got to hurry.

MARY: Name one point.

DIANE: You've got nice hands.

MARY (*Surprised*): Do I?

DIANE: Very nice hands.

MARY: Do I really?

DIANE: Hands are very important.

(MARY *shows her hands to the mirror and gives them little exercises.*)

DIANE: Men often look at hands.

MARY: They do?

DIANE: Often.

MARY: What do they think?

DIANE: Think?

MARY (*Impatiently*): When they look at hands.

DIANE: They think: There's a nice pair of hands.

MARY: What else?

DIANE: They think: Those are nice hands to hold.

MARY: And?

DIANE: They think: Those are nice hands to—squeeze.

MARY: I'm listening.

DIANE: They think: Those are nice hands to—kiss.

MARY: Go on.

DIANE: They think—(*racking her brain for compassion's sake.*)

MARY: Well?

| 147

DIANE: Those are nice hands to—love!

MARY: Love!

DIANE: Yes.

MARY: What do you mean "love"?

DIANE: I don't have to explain.

MARY: Someone is going to love my hands?

DIANE: Yes.

MARY: What about my arms?

DIANE: What about them? (*A little surly.*)

MARY: Are they one of my points?
(*Pause.*)

DIANE: I suppose not one of your best.

MARY: What about my shoulders?
(*Pause.*)

DIANE: Your shoulders are all right.

MARY: You know they're not. They're not.

DIANE: Then what did you ask me for?

MARY: What about my bosom?

DIANE: I don't know your bosom.

MARY: You do know my bosom.

DIANE: I don't.

MARY: You do.

DIANE: I do not know your bosom.

MARY: You've seen me undressed.

DIANE: I never looked that hard.

MARY: You know my bosom all right. (*But she'll let it pass. She looks disgustedly at her hands.*)

MARY: Hands!

DIANE: Don't be so hard on yourself.

MARY: Sexiest knuckles on the block.

DIANE: Why hurt yourself?

MARY: My fingers are really stacked.

DIANE: Stop, sweetie.

MARY: They come when they shake hands with me.

DIANE: Now please!

MARY: You don't know how it feels.
        (*Pause.*)

MARY: Just tell me what it's like.

DIANE: What like?

MARY: To be beautiful. You've never told me.

DIANE: There's no such thing as beautiful.

MARY: Sure.

DIANE: It's how you feel.

MARY: I'm going to believe that.

DIANE: It's how you feel makes you beautiful.

MARY: Do you know how I feel?

DIANE: Don't tell me.

MARY: Ugly.

DIANE: You don't have to talk like that.

MARY: I feel ugly. What does that make me?
        (**DIANE** *declines to answer. She steps into her high-heeled shoes, the elevation bringing out the harder lines of her legs, adding to her stature an appealing haughtiness and to her general beauty a touch of violence.*)

MARY: According to what you said.

DIANE: I don't know.

MARY: You said: It's how you feel makes you beautiful.

DIANE: I know what I said.

MARY: I feel ugly. So what does that make me?

DIANE: I don't know.

MARY: According to what you said.

DIANE: I don't know.

MARY: Don't be afraid to say it.

DIANE: Harry will be here.

MARY: Say it! (*Launching herself into hysteria.*)

DIANE: I've got to get ready.

MARY: You never say it. You're afraid to say it. It won't kill you. The word won't kill you. You think it but you won't say it. When you get up in the morning you tiptoe to the bathroom. I tiptoe to the bathroom but I sound like an army. What do you think I think when I hear myself? Don't you think I know the difference? It's no secret. It's not as though there aren't any mirrors. If you only said it I wouldn't try. I don't want to try. I don't want to have to try. If you only once said I was—ugly!

(DIANE *comforts her.*)

DIANE: You're not ugly, sweetie. Nobody's ugly. Everybody can be beautiful. Your turn will come. Your man will come. He'll take you in his arms. No no no, you're not ugly. He'll teach you that you are beautiful. Then you'll know what it is.

(*Cradling her.*)

MARY: Will he?

DIANE: Of course he will.

MARY: Until then?

DIANE: You've got to keep going, keep looking.

MARY: Keep up with my exercises.

DIANE: Yes.

MARY: Keep up with my ballet lessons.

DIANE: Exactly.

MARY: Try and lose weight.

DIANE: Follow the book.

MARY: Brush my hair the right way.

DIANE: That's the spirit.

MARY: A hundred strokes.

DIANE: Good.

MARY: I've got to gain confidence.

DIANE: You will.

MARY: I can't give up.

DIANE: It's easier than you think.

MARY: Concentrate on my best points.

DIANE: Make the best of what you have.

MARY: Why not start now?

DIANE: Why not.

(MARY *gathers herself together, checks her posture in the mirror, crosses to the record-player and switches it on. "The Dance of the Sugar-plum Fairy." She begins the ballet exercises she has learned, perhaps, at the YWCA, two evenings a week. Between the final touches of her toilet* DIANE *encourages her with nods of approval. The doorbell rings. Enter* HARRY *in evening clothes, glittering although his expression is solemn, for he has come on an important mission.*)

HARRY: Hi girls. Don't mind me, Mary.

(MARY *waves in the midst of a difficult contortion.*)

DIANE: Darling!

(DIANE *sweeps into his arms, takes the attitude of a dancing partner.* HARRY, *with a trace of reluctance, consents to lead her in a ballroom step across the floor.*)

HARRY: I've got something on my mind.

> (DIANE *squeezes his arm, disengages herself, crosses to* MARY *and whispers.*)

DIANE: He's got something on his mind.

> (DIANE *and* MARY *embrace in the usual squeaky conspiratorial manner with which girls preface happy matrimonial news. While* MARY *smiles benignly exeunt* HARRY *and* DIANE. MARY *turns the machine louder, moves in front of the mirror, resumes the ballet exercises. She stops them from time to time to check various parts of her anatomy in the mirror at close range, as if the effects of the discipline might be already apparent.*)

MARY: Goody.

> (*A long determined ring of the doorbell.* MARY *stops, eyes bright with expectation. Perhaps the miracle is about to unfold. She smooths her dress and hair, switches off the machine, opens the door.* THE COLLECTOR *enters with lumbering difficulty, looks around, takes control. The power she radiates is somehow guaranteed by her grotesque form. Her body is a huge damaged tank operating under the intimate command of a brilliant field warrior which is her mind:* MARY *waits, appalled and intimidated.*)

COLLECTOR: I knew there was people in because I heard music. (MARY *cannot speak.*) Some people don't like to open the door. I'm in charge of the whole block.

MARY (*Recovering*): Are you collecting for something?

COLLECTOR:	The United Fund for the Obese, you know, UFO. That includes The Obese Catholic Drive, The Committee for Jewish Fat People, the Help the Blind Obese, and the Universal Aid to the Obese. If you make one donation you won't be bothered again.
MARY:	We've never been asked before.
COLLECTOR:	I know. But I have your card now. The whole Fund has been reorganized.
MARY:	It has?
COLLECTOR:	Oh yes. Actually it was my idea to have the Obese themselves go out and canvass. They were against it at first but I convinced them. It's the only fair way. Gives the public an opportunity to see exactly where their money goes. And I've managed to get the Spastic and Polio and Cancer people to see the light. It's the only fair way. We're all over the neighbourhood.
MARY:	It's very—courageous.
COLLECTOR:	That's what my husband says.
MARY:	Your husband!
COLLECTOR:	He'd prefer me to stay at home. Doesn't believe in married girls working.
MARY:	Have—have you been married long?
COLLECTOR:	Just short of a year. (*Coyly.*) You might say we're still honeymooners.
MARY:	Oh.
COLLECTOR:	Don't be embarrassed. One of the aims of our organization is to help people like me lead normal lives. Now what could be more normal than marriage? Can you

think of anything more normal? Of course you can't. It makes you feel less isolated, part of the whole community. Our people are getting married all the time.

MARY: Of course, of course. (*She is disintegrating.*)

COLLECTOR: I didn't think it would work out myself at first. But John is so loving. He's taken such patience with me. When we're together it's as though there's nothing wrong with me at all.

MARY: What does your husband do?

COLLECTOR: He's a chef.

MARY: A chef.

COLLECTOR: Not in any famous restaurant. Just an ordinary chef. But it's good enough for me. Sometimes, when he's joking, he says I married him for his profession. (MARY *tries to laugh.*) Well I've been chatting too long about myself and I have the rest of this block to cover. How much do you think you'd like to give. I know you're a working girl.

MARY: I don't know, I really don't know.

COLLECTOR: May I make a suggestion?

MARY: Of course.

COLLECTOR: Two dollars.

MARY: Two dollars. (*Goes to her purse obediently.*)

COLLECTOR: I don't think that's too much, do you?

MARY: No no.

COLLECTOR: Five dollars would be too much.

MARY: Too much.

COLLECTOR: And one dollar just doesn't seem right.

MARY: Oh, I only have a five. I don't have any change.

COLLECTOR: I'll take it.

MARY: You'll take it?

COLLECTOR: I'll take it. (*A command.*)

(MARY *drops the bill in the transaction, being afraid to make any physical contact with* THE COLLECTOR. MARY *stoops to pick it up.* THE COLLECTOR *prevents her.*)

COLLECTOR: Let me do that. The whole idea is not to treat us like invalids. You just watch how well I get along. (THE COLLECTOR *retrieves the money with immense difficulty.*)

COLLECTOR: That wasn't so bad, was it?

MARY: No. Oh no. It wasn't so bad.

COLLECTOR: I've even done a little dancing in my time.

MARY: That's nice.

COLLECTOR: They have courses for us. First we do it in water, but very soon we're right up there on dry land. I bet you do some dancing yourself, a girl like you. I heard music when I came.

MARY: Not really.

COLLECTOR: Do you know what would make me very happy?

MARY: It's very late.

COLLECTOR: To see you do a step or two.

MARY: I'm quite tired.

COLLECTOR: A little whirl.

MARY: I'm not very good.

COLLECTOR: A whirl, a twirl, a bit of a swing. I'll put
             it on for you.

             (THE COLLECTOR *begins to make her way
             to the record-player.* MARY, *who cannot
             bear to see her expend herself, overtakes
             her and switches it on.* MARY *performs
             for a few moments while* THE COLLECTOR
             *looks on with pleasure, tapping out the
             time.* MARY *breaks off the dance.*)

MARY: I'm not very good.

COLLECTOR: Would a little criticism hurt you?

MARY: No—

COLLECTOR: They're not dancing like that any more.

MARY: No?

COLLECTOR: They're doing something altogether dif-
             ferent.

MARY: I wouldn't know.

COLLECTOR: More like this.

             (*The record has reached the end of its
             spiral and is now jerking back and forth
             over the last few bars.*)

COLLECTOR: Don't worry about that.

             (THE COLLECTOR *moves to stage centre
             and executes a terrifying dance to the re-
             peating bars of music. It combines the
             heavy mechanical efficiency of a printing
             machine with the convulsions of a spas-
             tic. It could be a garbage heap falling
             down an escalator. It is grotesque but
             military, excruciating but triumphant.
             It is a woman-creature proclaiming a
             disease of the flesh.* MARY *tries to look*

156 |

away but cannot. She stares, dumb-
founded, shattered, and ashamed.)

COLLECTOR: We learn to get around, don't we?

MARY: It's very nice. (*She switches off the ma-*
chine.)

COLLECTOR: That's more what they're doing.

MARY: Is it?

COLLECTOR: In most of the places. A few haven't
caught on.

MARY: I'm very tired now. I think—

COLLECTOR: You must be tired.

MARY: I am.

COLLECTOR: With all my talking.

MARY: Not really.

COLLECTOR: I've taken your time.

MARY: You haven't.

COLLECTOR: I'll write you a receipt.

MARY: It isn't necessary.

COLLECTOR: Yes it is. (*She writes.*) This isn't official.
An official receipt will be mailed to you
from Fund headquarters. You'll need it
for Income Tax.

MARY: Thank you.

COLLECTOR: Thank *you*. I've certainly enjoyed this.

MARY: Me too. (*She is now confirmed in a state
of numbed surrender.*)

COLLECTOR (*with a sudden disarming tenderness that
changes through the speech into a vision
of uncompromising domination*): No,
you didn't. Oh, I know you didn't. It
frightened you. It made you sort of sick.
It had to frighten you. It always does at
the beginning. Everyone is frightened at

| 157

the beginning. That's part of it. Frightened and—fascinated. Fascinated—that's the important thing. You were fascinated too, and that's why I know you'll learn the new step. You see, it's a way to start over and forget about all the things you were never really good at. Nobody can resist that, can they? That's why you'll learn the new step. That's why I must teach you. And soon you'll want to learn. Everybody will want to learn. We'll be teaching everybody.

MARY: I'm fairly busy.

COLLECTOR: Don't worry about that. We'll find time. We'll make time. You won't believe this now, but soon, and it will be very soon, you're going to want me to teach you everything. Well, you better get some sleep. Sleep is very important. I want to say thank you. All the Obese want to say thank you.

MARY: Nothing. Good night.

COLLECTOR: Just beginning for us.

(*Exit* THE COLLECTOR. MARY, *dazed and exhausted, stands at the door for some time. She moves toward stage centre, attempts a few elementary exercises, collapses into the chair and stares dumbly at the audience. The sound of a key in the lock. Door opens. Enter* DIANE *alone, crying.*)

DIANE: I didn't want him to see me home.

(MARY *is unable to cope with anyone else's problem at this point.*)

MARY: What's the matter with you?

DIANE: It's impossible.

MARY: What's impossible?

DIANE: What happened.

MARY: What happened?

DIANE: He doesn't want to see me any more.

MARY: Harry?

DIANE: Harry.

MARY: Your Harry?

DIANE: You know damn well which Harry.

MARY: Doesn't want to see you any more?

DIANE: No.

MARY: I thought he loved you.

DIANE: So did I.

MARY: I thought he really loved you.

DIANE: So did I.

MARY: You told me he said he loved you.

DIANE: He did.

MARY: But now he doesn't?

DIANE: No.

MARY: Oh.

DIANE: It's terrible.

MARY: It must be.

DIANE: It came so suddenly.

MARY: It must have.

DIANE: I thought he loved me.

MARY: So did I.

DIANE: He doesn't!

MARY: Don't cry.

DIANE: He's getting married.

MARY: He isn't!

DIANE: Yes.

MARY: He isn't!

DIANE: This Sunday.

MARY:	This Sunday?
DIANE:	Yes.
MARY:	So soon?
DIANE:	Yes.
MARY:	He told you that?
DIANE:	Tonight.
MARY:	What did he say?
DIANE:	He said he's getting married this Sunday.
MARY:	He's a bastard.
DIANE:	Don't say that.
MARY:	I say he's a bastard.
DIANE:	Don't talk that way.
MARY:	Why not?
DIANE:	Don't.
MARY:	After what he's done?
DIANE:	It's not his fault.
MARY:	Not his fault?
DIANE:	He fell in love.
	(*The word has its magic effect.*)
MARY:	Fell in *love*?
DIANE:	Yes.
MARY:	With someone else?
DIANE:	Yes.
MARY:	He fell out of love with you?
DIANE:	I suppose so.
MARY:	That's terrible.
DIANE:	He said he couldn't help it.
MARY:	Not if it's love.
DIANE:	He said it was.
MARY:	Then he couldn't help it.
	(DIANE *begins to remove her make-up and undress, reversing exactly every step of her toilet.* MARY, *still bewildered, but out of habit, assists her.*)

MARY: And you're so beautiful.
DIANE: No.
MARY: Your hair.
DIANE: No.
MARY: Your shoulders.
DIANE: No.
MARY: Everything.
(*Pause.*)
MARY: What did he say?
DIANE: He told me everything.
MARY: Such as what?
DIANE: Harry's a gentleman.
MARY: I always thought so.
DIANE: He wanted me to know everything.
MARY: It's only fair.
DIANE: He told me about her.
MARY: What did he say?
DIANE: He said he loves her.
MARY: Then he had no choice.
DIANE: He said she's beautiful.
MARY: He didn't!
DIANE: What can you expect?
MARY: I suppose so.
DIANE: He loves her, after all.
MARY: Then I guess he thinks she's beautiful.
(*Pause.*)
MARY: What else did he say?
DIANE: He told me everything.
MARY: How did he meet her?
DIANE: She came to his house.
MARY: What for?
DIANE: She was collecting money.
MARY: Money! (*Alarm.*)
DIANE: For a charity.

MARY: Charity!

DIANE: Invalids of some kind.

MARY: Invalids!

DIANE: That's the worst part.

MARY: What part?

DIANE: She's that way herself.

MARY: What way?

DIANE: You know.

MARY: What way, what way?

DIANE: You know.

MARY: Say it!

DIANE: She's an invalid.

MARY: Harry's marrying an invalid?

DIANE: This Sunday.

MARY: You said he said she was beautiful.

DIANE: He did.

MARY: Harry is going to marry an invalid.

DIANE: What should I do?

MARY: Harry who said he loved you. (*Not a question.*)

DIANE: I'm miserable.

(MARY *is like a woman moving through a fog toward a light.*)

MARY: Harry is going to marry an invalid. He thinks she's beautiful.

(MARY *switches on the record-player.*) She came to his door. Harry who told you he loved you. You who told me I had my points.

(*"The Dance of the Sugar-plum Fairy" begins.* MARY *dances but she does not use the steps she learned at the YWCA. She dances in conscious imitation of* THE COLLECTOR.)

DIANE: What are you doing? (*Horrified.*)
         (MARY *smiles at her.*)
DIANE: Stop it! Stop it this instant!
MARY: Don't tell me what to do. Don't you dare.
         Don't ever tell me what to do. Don't ever.
         (*The dance continues.* DIANE, *dressed in
         bra and panties as at the beginning,
         backs away.*)

CURTAIN

Toronto has been good to me
I relaxed on TV
I attacked several dead horses
I spread rumours about myself
I reported a Talmudic quarrel
    with the Montreal Jewish Community
I forged a death certificate
    in case I had to disappear
I listened to a huckster
    welcome me to the world
I slept behind my new sunglasses
I abandoned the care of my pimples
I dreamed that I needed nobody
I faced my trap
I withheld my opinion on matters
    on which I had no opinion
I humoured the rare January weather
    with a jaunty step for the sake of heroism
Not very carefully
    I thought about the future
and how little I know about animals
The future seemed unnecessarily black and strong
as if it had received my casual mistakes
through a carbon sheet

WHY DID YOU GIVE MY NAME
TO THE POLICE?

You recited the Code of Comparisons
in your mother's voice.
Again you were the blue-robed seminary girl
but these were not poplar trees and nuns
you walked between.
These were Laws.
Damn you for making this moment hopeless,
now, as a clerk in uniform fills
in my father's name.

You too must find the moment hopeless
in the Tennyson Hotel.
I know your stomach.
The brass bed bearing your suitcase
rumbles away like an automatic
promenading target in a shooting gallery:
you stand with your hands full
of a necklace you wanted to pack.
In detail you recall your rich dinner.
Grab that towel rack!

Doesn't the sink seem a fraud
with its hair-swirled pipes?
Doesn't the overhead bulb
seem burdened with mucus?
Things will be better at City Hall.

Now you must learn to read
newspapers without laughing.
No hysterical headline breakfasts.
Police be your Guard,

Telephone Book your Brotherhood.
Action! Action! Action!
Goodbye Citizen.

The clerk is talking to nobody.
Do you see how I have tiptoed
out of his brown file?
He fingers his uniform
like a cheated bargain hunter.
Answer me, please talk to me, he weeps,
say I'm not a doorman.

I plug the wires of your fear
(ah, this I was always meant to do)
into the lust-asylum universe:
raped by aimless old electricity
you stiffen over the steel books of your bed
like a fish
in a liquid air experiment.
Thus withers the Civil Triumph
(Laws rush in to corset the collapse)
for you are mistress to the Mayor,
he electrocuted in your frozen juices.

THE MUSIC CREPT BY US

I would like to remind
the management
that the drinks are watered
and the hat-check girl
has syphilis
and the band is composed
of former SS monsters
However since it is
New Year's Eve
and I have lip cancer
I will place my
paper hat on my
concussion and dance

DISGUISES

I am sorry that the rich man must go
and his house become a hospital.
I loved his wine, his contemptuous servants,
his ten-year-old ceremonies.
I loved his car which he wore like a snail's shell
everywhere, and I loved his wife,
the hours she put into her skin,
the milk, the lust, the industries
that served her complexion.
I loved his son who looked British
but had American ambitions
and let the word aristocrat comfort him
like a reprieve while Kennedy reigned.
I loved the rich man: I hate to see
his season ticket for the Opera
fall into a pool for opera-lovers.

I am sorry that the old worker must go
who called me mister when I was twelve
and sir when I was twenty
who studied against me in obscure socialist
clubs which met in restaurants.
I loved the machine he knew like a wife's body.
I loved his wife who trained bankers
in an underground pantry
and never wasted her ambition in ceramics.
I loved his children who debate
and come first at McGill University.
Goodbye old gold-watch winner
all your complex loyalties
must now be borne by one-faced patriots.

Goodbye dope fiends of North Eastern Lunch
circa 1948, your spoons which were not
Swedish Stainless, were the same colour
as the hoarded clasps and hooks
of discarded soiled therapeutic corsets.
I loved your puns about snow
even if they lasted the full seven-month
Montreal winter. Go write your memoirs
for the Psychedelic Review.

Goodbye sex fiends of Beaver Pond
who dreamed of being jacked-off
by electric milking machines.
You had no Canada Council.
You had to open little boys
with a pen-knife.
I loved your statement to the press:
"I didn't think he'd mind."
Goodbye articulate monsters
Abbott and Costello have met Frankenstein.

I am sorry that the conspirators must go
the ones who scared me by showing me
a list of all the members of my family.
I loved the way they reserved judgement
about Genghis Khan. They loved me because
I told them their little beards
made them dead-ringers for Lenin.
The bombs went off in Westmount
and now they are ashamed
like a successful outspoken Schopenhauerian
whose room-mate has committed suicide.
Suddenly they are all making movies.
I have no one to buy coffee for.

I embrace the changeless:
the committed men in public wards
oblivious as Hassidim
who believe that they are someone else.
Bravo! Abelard, viva! Rockefeller,
have these buns, Napoleon,
hurrah! betrayed Duchess.
Long live you chronic self-abusers!
you monotheists!
you familiars of the Absolute
sucking at circles!
You are all my comfort
as I turn to face the beehive
as I disgrace my style
as I coarsen my nature
as I invent jokes
as I pull up my garters
as I accept responsibility.

You comfort me
incorrigible betrayers of the self
as I salute fashion
and bring my mind
    like a promiscuous air-hostess
handing out parachutes in a nose dive
bring my butchered mind
to bear upon the facts.

LOT

Give me back my house
Give me back my young wife
    I shouted to the sunflower in my path
Give me back my scalpel
Give me back my mountain view
    I said to the seeds along my path
Give me back my name
Give me back my childhood list
    I whispered to the dust when the path gave out
Now sing
Now sing
    sang my master as I waited in the raw wind
Have I come so far for this
    I wondered as I waited in the pure cold
    ready at last to argue for my silence
Tell me master
do my lips move
or where does it come from
    this soft total chant that drives my soul
    like a spear of salt into the rock
Give me back my house
Give me back my young wife

ONE OF THE NIGHTS I
DIDN'T KILL MYSELF

You dance on the day you saved
my theoretical angels
daughters of the new middle-class
who wear your mouths like Bardot
    Come my darlings
the movies are true
I am the lost sweet singer whose death
in the fog your new high-heeled boots
have ground into cigarette butts
I was walking the harbour this evening
looking for a 25-cent bed of water
but I will sleep tonight
with your garters curled in my shoes
like rainbows on vacation
with your virginity ruling
the condom cemeteries like a 2nd chance
I believe I believe
Thursday December 12th
is not the night
and I will kiss again the slope of a breast
little nipple above me
like a sunset

BULLETS

Listen all you bullets
that never hit:
a lot of throats are growing
in open collars
like frozen milk bottles
on a 5 a.m. street
throats that are waiting
for bite scars
but will settle
for bullet holes

You restless bullets
lost in swarms
from undecided wars:
fasten on
these nude throats
that need some
decoration

I've done my own work:
I had 3 jewels
no more
and I have placed them
on my choices
jewels
although they performed
like bullets:
an instant of ruby
before the hands
came up
to stem the mess

And you over there
my little acrobat:
swing fast
After me
there is no care
and the air
is heavily armed
and has
the wildest aim

THE BIG WORLD

The big world will find out
about this farm
the big world will learn
the details of what
I worked out in the can

And your curious life with me
will be told so often
that no one will believe
you grew old

FRONT LAWN

The snow was falling
over my penknife
There was a movie
in the fireplace
The apples were wrapped
in 8-year-old blond hair
Starving and dirty
the janitor's daughter never
turned up in November
to pee from her sweet crack
on the gravel
    I'll go back one day
when my cast is off
Elm leaves are falling
over my bow and arrow
Candy is going bad
and Boy Scout calendars
are on fire
    My old mother
sits in her Cadillac
laughing her Danube laugh
as I tell her that we own
all the worms
under our front lawn
    Rust rust rust
in the engines of love and time

KERENSKY

My friend walks through our city this winter night,
fur-hatted, whistling, anti-mediterranean,
stricken with seeing Eternity in all that is seasonal.
He is the Kerensky of our Circle
always about to chair the last official meeting
before the pros take over, they of the pure smiling eyes
trained only for Form.

    He knows there are no measures to guarantee
the Revolution, or to preserve the row of muscular icicles
which will chart Winter's decline like a graph.

    There is nothing for him to do but preside
over the last official meeting.
It will all come round again: the heartsick teachers
who make too much of poetry, their students
who refuse to suffer, the cache of rifles in the lawyer's attic:
and then the magic, the 80-year comet touching
the sturdiest houses. The Elite Corps commits suicide
in the tennis-ball basement. Poets ride buses free.
The General insists on a popularity poll. Troops study satire.
A strange public generosity prevails.

    Only too well he knows the tiny moment when
everything is possible, when pride is loved, beauty held
in common, like having an exquisite sister,
and a man gives away his death like a piece of advice.

    Our Kerensky has waited for these moments
over a table in a rented room
when poems grew like butterflies on the garbage of his life.
How many times? The sad answer is: they can be counted.
Possible and brief: this is his vision of Revolution.

    Who will parade the shell today?
Who will kill in the name
of the husk? Who will write a Law to raise the corpse

which cries now only for weeds and excrement?
See him walk the streets, the last guard, the only idler
on the square. He must keep the wreck of the Revolution
the debris of public beauty
from the pure smiling eyes of the trained visionaries
who need our daily lives perfect.

The soft snow begins to honour him with epaulets, and to provoke the animal past of his fur hat. He wears a death, but he allows the snow, like an ultimate answer, to forgive him, just for this jewelled moment of his coronation. The carved gargoyles of the City Hall receive the snow as bibs beneath their drooling lips. How they resemble the men of profane vision, the same greed, the same intensity as they who whip their minds to recall an ancient lucky orgasm, yes, yes, he knows that deadly concentration, they are the founders, they are the bankers—of History! He rests in his walk as they consume of the generous night everything that he does not need.

ANOTHER NIGHT WITH TELESCOPE

Come back to me
            brutal empty room
Thin Byzantine face
        preside over this new fast
I am broken with easy grace
Let me be neither
            father nor child
but one who spins
on an eternal unimportant loom
        patterns of wars and grass
which do not last the night
            I know the stars
are wild as dust
and wait for no man's discipline
            but as they wheel
from sky to sky they rake
        our lives with pins of light

IV / Parasites of Heaven

THE NIGHTMARES DO NOT SUDDENLY

The nightmares do not suddenly
develop happy endings
          I merely step out of them
as a five-year-old scientist
leaves the room
where he has dissected an alarm clock

Love wears out
like overused mirrors unsilvering
          and parts of your faces
make room for the wall behind
If terror needs my round green eyes
for a masterpiece
          let it lure them with nude keyholes
mounted on an egg

And should Love decide
I am not the one
          to stand scratching his head
wondering what wall to lean on
          send King Farouk to argue
or come to me dressed as a fast

A CROSS DIDN'T FALL ON ME

A cross didn't fall on me
when I went for hot-dogs
and the all-night Greek
slave in the Silver Gameland
didn't think I was his brother
Love me because nothing happens

I believe the rain will not
make me feel like a feather
when it comes tonight after
the streetcars have stopped
because my size is definite
Love me because nothing happens

Do you have any idea how
many movies I had to watch
before I knew surely
that I would love you
when the lights woke up
Love me because nothing happens

Here is a headline July 14
in the city of Montreal
Intervention décisive de Pearson
à la conférence du Commonwealth
That was yesterday
Love me because nothing happens

Stars and stars and stars
keep it to themselves
Have you ever noticed how private
a wet tree is

a curtain of razor blades
Love me because nothing happens

Why should I be alone
if what I say is true
I confess I mean to find
a passage or forge a passport
or talk a new language
Love me because nothing happens

I confess I meant to grow
wings and lose my mind
I confess that I've
forgotten what for
Why wings and a lost mind
Love me because nothing happens

SO YOU'RE THE KIND OF VEGETARIAN

So you're the kind of vegetarian
that only eats roses
Is that what you mean
with your Beautiful Losers

1965

Nothing has been broken
  though one of the links of the chain
is a blue butterfly

Here he was attacked
  They smiled as they came and retired
baffled with blue dust

The banks so familiar with metal
  they made for the wings
The thick vaults fluttered

The pretty girls advanced
  their fingers cupped
They bled from the mouth as though struck

The jury asked for pity
  and touched and were electrocuted
by the blue antennae

A thrust at any link
  might have brought him down
but each of you aimed at the blue butterfly

HERE WE ARE AT THE WINDOW

Here we are at the window. Great unbound sheaves of rain wandering across the mountain, parades of wind and driven silver grass. So long I've tried to give a name to freedom, today my freedom lost its name, like a student's room travelling into the morning with its lights still on. Every act has its own style of freedom, whatever that means. Now I'm commanded to think of weeds, to worship the strong weeds that grew through the night, green and wet, the white thread roots taking lottery orders from the coils of brain mud, the permeable surface of the world. Did you know that the brain developed out of a fold in the epidermis? Did you? Falling ribbons of silk, the length of rivers, cross the face of the mountain, systems of grass and cable. Freedom lost its name to the style with which things happen. The straight trees, the spools of weed, the travelling skeins of rain floating through the folds of the mountain—here we are at the window. Are you ready now? Have I dismissed myself? May I fire from the hip? Brothers, each at your window, we are the style of so much passion, we are the order of style, we are pure style called to delight a fold of the sky.

CLEAN AS THE GRASS FROM WHICH

Clean as the grass from which
the sun has burned the little dew
I come to this page
in the not so early morning
with a picture of him
whom I could not be for long
not wanting to return or begin
again the idolatry of terror

He was burned away from me
by needles by ashes
by various shames I
engineered against his innocence
by documenting the love of one
who gathered my first songs
and gave her body to my wandering

With a picture of him
grooming her thighs for a journey
with a picture of him
buying her a staring peacock feather
with a picture of him
knighted by her smile her soft fatigue
I begin the hopeless formula
she already had the gold from

Live for him huge black eyes
He never understood their purity
or how they watched him prepare
to ditch the early songs and say goodbye
Sleep beside him uncaptured darling
while I fold into a kite

the long evenings he scratched with
experiments the empty dazzling mornings
that forbid me to recall your name

With a picture of him
standing by the window while she slept
with a picture of him
wondering what adventure is
wondering what cruelty is
with a picture of him
waking her with an angry kiss
leading her body into use and time
I bargain with the fire
which must ignore the both of them

WHEN I PAID THE SUN TO RUN

When I paid the sun to run
It ran and I sat down and cried
The sun I spent my money on
Went round and round inside
The world all at once
Charged with insignificance

I SEE YOU ON A GREEK MATTRESS

I see you on a Greek mattress
reading the *Book of Changes,*
Lebanese candy in the air.
On the whitewashed wall I see
you raise another hexagram
for the same old question:
how can you be free?
I see you cleaning your pipe
with the hairpin
of somebody's innocent night.
I see the plastic Evil Eye
pinned to your underwear.
Once again you throw the pennies,
once again you read
how the pieces of the world
have changed around your question.
Did you get to the Himalayas?
Did you visit that monk in New Jersey?
I never answered any of your letters.
Oh Steve, do you remember me?

1963

SUZANNE WEARS A LEATHER COAT

Suzanne wears a leather coat.
Her legs are insured by many burnt bridges.
Her calves are full as spinnakers
in a clean race, hard from following music
beyond the maps of any audience.

Suzanne wears a leather coat
because she is not a civilian.
She never walks casually down Ste Catherine
because with every step she must redeem
the clubfoot crowds and stalk the field
of huge hail-stones that never melted,
I mean the cemetery.

Stand up! stand!
Suzanne is walking by.
She wears a leather coat. She won't stop
to bandage the fractures she walks between.
She must not stop, she must not
carry money.
Many are the workers in charity.

Few serve the lilac,
few heal with mist.
Suzanne wears a leather coat.
Her breasts yearn for marble.
The traffic halts: people fall out
of their cars. None of their most drooling

thoughts are wild enough
to build the ant-full crystal city
she would splinter with the tone of her step.

1963

ONE NIGHT I BURNED THE HOUSE I LOVED

One night I burned the house I loved,
It lit a perfect ring
In which I saw some weeds and stone
Beyond—not anything.

Certain creatures of the air
Frightened by the night,
They came to see the world again
And perished in the light.

Now I sail from sky to sky
And all the blackness sings
Against the boat that I have made
Of mutilated wings.

TWO WENT TO SLEEP

Two went to sleep
almost every night
one dreamed of mud
one dreamed of Asia
visiting a zeppelin
visiting Nijinsky
Two went to sleep
one dreamed of ribs
one dreamed of senators
Two went to sleep
two travellers
The long marriage
in the dark
The sleep was old
the travellers were old
one dreamed of oranges
one dreamed of Carthage
Two friends asleep
years locked in travel
Good night my darling
as the dreams waved goodbye
one travelled lightly
one walked through water
visiting a chess game
visiting a booth
always returning
to wait out the day
One carried matches
one climbed a beehive
one sold an earphone
one shot a German

Two went to sleep
every sleep went together
wandering away
from an operating table
one dreamed of grass
one dreamed of spokes
one bargained nicely
one was a snowman
one counted medicine
one tasted pencils
one was a child
one was a traitor
visiting heavy industry
visiting the family
Two went to sleep
none could foretell
one went with baskets
one took a ledger
one night happy
one night in terror
Love could not bind them
Fear could not either
they went unconnected
they never knew where
always returning
to wait out the day
parting with kissing
parting with yawns
visiting Death till
they wore out their welcome
visiting Death till
the right disguise worked

1964

In the Bible generations pass in a paragraph, a betrayal is disposed of in a phrase, the creation of the world consumes a page. I could never pick the important dynasty out of a multitude, you must have your forehead shining to do that, or to choose out of the snarled network of daily evidence the denials and the loyalties. Who can choose what olive tree the story will need to shade its lovers, what tree out of the huge orchard will give them the particular view of branches and sky which will unleash their kisses. Only two shining people know, they go directly to the roots they lie between. For my part I describe the whole orchard.

FOUND ONCE AGAIN SHAMELESSLY
IGNORING THE SWANS ...

Found once again shamelessly ignoring the swans who in-
flame the spectators on the shores of American rivers; found
once again allowing the juicy contract to expire because the
telephone has a magic correspondence with my tapeworm;
found once again leaving the garlanded manhood in danger
of long official repose while it is groomed for marble in
seedily historic back rooms; found once again humiliating
the bank clerk with eye-to-eye wrestling, art dogma, lives
that loaf and stare, and other stage whispers of genius;
found once again the chosen object of heavenly longing
such as can ambush a hermit in a forest with visions of a
busy parking lot; found once again smelling mothball
sweaters, titling home movies, untangling Victorian salmon
rods, fanatically convinced that a world of sporty order is
just around the corner; found once again planning the ideal
lonely year which waits like first flesh love on a calendar of
third choices; found once again hovering like a twine-eating
kite over hands that feed me, verbose under the influence
of astrology; found one again selling out to accessible local
purity while Pentagon Tiffany evil alone can guarantee my
power; found once again trusting that my friends grew up
in Eden and will not harm me when at last I am armourless
and absolutely silent; found once again at the very beginning, veteran of several useless ordeals, prophetic but not
seminal, the purist for the masses of tomorrow; found once
again sweetening life which I have abandoned, like a fired
zoo-keeper sneaking peanuts to publicized sodomized ele-
phants; found once again flaunting the rainbow which
demonstrates that I am permitted only that which I urgently
need; found once again cleansing my tongue of all possibilities, of all possibilities but my perfect one.

1964

WHEN I HEAR YOU SING

When I hear you sing
Solomon
animal throat, eyes beaming
sex and wisdom
My hands ache from

I left blood on the doors of my home
Solomon
I am very alone from aiming songs
at God for
I thought that beside me there was no one
Solomon

HE WAS LAME

He was lame
as a 3 legged dog
screamed as he came
through the fog

If you are the Light
give me a light
buddy

1965

I AM TOO LOUD WHEN YOU ARE GONE

I am too loud when you are gone
I am John the Baptist, cheated by mere water
and merciful love, wild but over-known
John of honey, of time, longing not for
music, longing, longing to be Him
I am diminished, I peddle versions of Word
that don't survive the tablets broken stone
I am alone when you are gone

Somewhere in my trophy room the crucifixion and other sacrifices were still going on, but the flesh and nails were grown over with rust and I could not tell where the flesh ended and the wood began or on which wall the instruments were hung.

I passed by limbs and faces arranged in this museum like hanging kitchen tools, and some brushed my arm as the hallway reeled me in, but I pocketed my hands along with some vulnerable smiles, and I continued on.

I heard the rooms behind me clamour an instant for my brain, and once the brain responded, out of habit, weakly, as if thinking someone else's history, and somewhere in that last tune it learned that it was not the Queen, it was a drone.

There ahead of me extended an impossible trophy: the bright, great sky, where no men lived. Beautiful and empty, now luminous with a splendour emanating from my own flesh, the tuneless sky washed and washed my lineless face and bathed in waves my heart like a red translucent stone. Until my eyes gave out I lived there as my home.

Today I know the only distance that I came was to the threshold of my trophy room. Among the killing instruments again I am further from sacrifice than when I began. I do not stare or plead with passing pilgrims to help me there. I call it discipline but perhaps it is fallen pride alone.

I'm not the one to learn an exercise for dwelling in the sky. My trophy room is vast and hung with crutches, ladders, braces, hooks. Unlike the invalid's cathedral, men hang with these instruments. A dancing wall of molecules, changing nothing, has cleared a place for me and my time.

YOU KNOW WHERE I HAVE BEEN

You know where I have been
Why my knees are raw
I'd like to speak to you
Who will see what I saw

Some men who saw me fall
Spread the news of failure
I want to speak to them
The dogs of literature

Pass me as I proudly
Passed the others
Who kneel in secret flight
Pass us proudly Brothers

I MET A WOMAN LONG AGO

I met a woman long ago,
hair black as black can go.
Are you a teacher of the heart?
Soft she answered No.

I met a girl across the sea,
hair the gold that gold can be.
Are you a teacher of the heart?
Yes, but not for thee.

I knew a man who lost his mind
in some lost place I wished to find.
Follow me, he said,
but he walked behind.

I walked into a hospital
Where none was sick and none was well.
When at night the nurses left,
I could not walk at all.

Not too slow, not too soon
morning came, then came noon.
Dinner time a scalpel blade
lay beside my spoon.

Some girls wander by mistake
into the mess that scalpels make.
Are you teachers of the heart?
We teach old hearts to break.

One day I woke up alone,
hospital and nurses gone.

Have I carved enough?
You are a bone.

I ate and ate and ate,
I didn't miss a plate.
How much do these suppers cost?
We'll take it out in hate.

I spent my hatred every place,
on every work, on every face.
Someone gave me wishes.
I wished for an embrace.

Several girls embraced me, then
I was embraced by men.
Is my passion perfect?
Do it once again.

I was handsome, I was strong,
I knew the words of every song.
Did my singing please you?
The words you sang were wrong.

Who are you whom I address?
Who takes down what I confess?
Are you a teacher of the heart?
A chorus answered Yes.

Teachers, are my lessons done
or must I learn another one?
They cried: Dear Sir or Madam,
Daughter, Son.

I'VE SEEN SOME LONELY HISTORY

I've seen some lonely history
The heart cannot explore
I've scratched some empty blackboards
They have no teachers for

I trailed my meagre demons
From Jerusalem to Rome
I had an invitation
But the host was not at home

There were contagious armies
That spread their uniform
To all parts of my body
Except where I was warm

And so I wore a helmet
With a secret neon sign
That lit up all the boundaries
So I could toe the line

My boots got very tired
Like a sentry's never should
I was walking on a tightrope
That was buried in the mud

Standing at the drugstore
It was very hard to learn
Though my name was everywhere
I had to wait my turn

I'm standing here before you
I don't know what I bring
If you can hear the music
Why don't you help me sing

SNOW IS FALLING

Snow is falling.
There is a nude in my room.
She surveys the wine-coloured carpet.

She is eighteen.
She has straight hair.
She speaks no Montreal language.

She doesn't feel like sitting down.
She shows no gooseflesh.
We can hear the storm.

She is lighting a cigarette
from the gas range.
She holds back her long hair.

1958

CREATED FIRES I CANNOT LOVE

Created fires I cannot love
lest I lose the ones above.
Poor enough, then I'll learn
to choose the fires where they burn.

O God, make me poor enough
to love your diamond in the rough,
or in my failure let me see
my greed raised to mystery.

Do you hate the ones who must
turn your world all to dust?
Do you hate the ones who ask
if Creation wears a mask?

God beyond the God I name,
if mask and fire are the same,
repair the seam my love leaps through,
uncreated fire to pursue.

Network of created fire,
maim my love and my desire.
Make me poor so I may be
servant in the world I see,

Or, as my love leaps wide,
confirm your servant in his pride:
if my love can't burn,
forbid a sickening return.

Is it here my love will train
not to leap so high again?

No praise here? no blame?
From my love you tear my name.

Unmake me as I'm washed
far from the fiery mask.
Gather my pride in the coded pain
which is also your domain.

CLAIM ME, BLOOD, IF YOU HAVE A STORY

Claim me, blood, if you have a story
to tell with my Jewish face,
you are strong and holy still, only
speak, like the Zohar, of a carved-out place
into which I must pour myself like wine,
an emptiness of history which I must seize
and occupy, calm and full in this confine,
becoming clear "like good wine on its lees."

1965

HE WAS BEAUTIFUL WHEN HE
SAT ALONE

He was beautiful when he sat alone, he was like me, he had wide lapels, he was holding the mug in the hardest possible way so that his fingers were all twisted but still long and beautiful, he didn't like to sit alone all the time, but this time, I swear, he didn't care one way or the other.

I'll tell you why I like to sit alone, because I'm a sadist, that's why we like to sit alone, because we're the sadists who like to sit alone.

He sat alone because he was beautifully dressed for the occasion and because he was not a civilian.

We are the sadists you don't have to worry about, you think, and we have no opinion on the matter of whether you have to worry about us, and we don't even like to think about the matter because it baffles us.

Maybe he doesn't mean a thing to me any more but I think he was like me.

You didn't expect to fall in love, I said to myself and at the same time I answered gently, Do you think so?

I heard you humming beautifully, your hum said that I can't ignore you, that I'd finally come around for a number of delicious reasons that only you knew about, and here I am, Miss Blood.

And you won't come back, you won't come back to where you left me, and that's why you keep my number, so you don't dial it by mistake when you're fooling with the dial not even dialing numbers.

You begin to bore us with your pain and we have decided to change your pain.

You said you were happiest when you danced, you said you were happiest when you danced with me, now which do you mean?

And so we changed his pain, we threw the idea of a body at him and we told him a joke, and then he thought a great deal about laughing and about the code.

And he thought that she thought that he thought that she thought that the worst thing a woman could do was to take a man away from his work because that made her what, ugly or beautiful?

And now you have entered the mathematical section of your soul which you claimed you never had. I suppose that this, plus the broken heart, makes you believe that now you have a perfect right to go out and tame the sadists.

He had the last line of each verse of the song but he didn't have any of the other lines, the last line was always the same, *Don't call yourself a secret unless you mean to keep it.*

He thought he knew, or he actually did know too much about singing to be a singer; and if there actually is such a condition, is anybody in it, and are sadists born there?

It is not a question mark, it is not an exclamation point, it is a full stop by the man who wrote Parasites of Heaven.

Even if we stated our case very clearly and all those who held as we do came to our side, all of them, we would still be very few.

1966

I AM A PRIEST OF GOD

I am a priest of God
I walk down the road
with my pockets in my hand
Sometimes I'm bad
then sometimes I'm very good
I believe that I believe
everything I should
I like to hear you say
when you dance with head rolling
upon a silver tray
that I am a priest of God

I thought I was doing 100 other things
but I was a priest of God
I loved 100 women
never told the same lie twice
I said O Christ you're selfish
but I shared my bread and rice
I heard my voice tell the crowd
that I was alone and a priest of God
making me so empty
that even now in 1966
I'm not sure I'm a priest of God

IN ALMOND TREES LEMON TREES

In almond trees lemon trees
wind and sun do as they please
Butterflies and laundry flutter
My love her hair is blond as butter

Wasps with yellow whiskers wait
for food beside her china plate
Ants beside her little feet
are there to share what she will eat

Who chopped down the bells that say
the world is born again today
We will feed you all my dears
this morning or in later years

SUZANNE TAKES YOU DOWN

Suzanne takes you down
to her place near the river,
you can hear the boats go by
you can stay the night beside her.
And you know that she's half crazy
but that's why you want to be there
and she feeds you tea and oranges
that come all the way from China.
Just when you mean to tell her
that you have no gifts to give her,
she gets you on her wave-length
and she lets the river answer
that you've always been her lover.
    And you want to travel with her,
    you want to travel blind
    and you know that she can trust you
    because you've touched her perfect body
    with your mind.

Jesus was a sailor
when he walked upon the water
and he spent a long time watching
from a lonely wooden tower
and when he knew for certain
only drowning men could see him
he said All men will be sailors then
until the sea shall free them,
but he himself was broken
long before the sky would open,
forsaken, almost human,
he sank beneath your wisdom like a stone.
    And you want to travel with him,

> you want to travel blind
> and you think maybe you'll trust him
> because he touched your perfect body
> with his mind.

Suzanne takes your hand
and she leads you to the river,
she is wearing rags and feathers
from Salvation Army counters.
The sun pours down like honey
on our lady of the harbour
as she shows you where to look
among the garbage and the flowers,
there are heroes in the seaweed
there are children in the morning,
they are leaning out for love
they will lean that way forever
while Suzanne she holds the mirror.
> And you want to travel with her
> and you want to travel blind
> and you're sure that she can find you
> because she's touched her perfect body
> with her mind.

GIVE ME BACK MY FINGERPRINTS

Give me back my fingerprints
My fingertips are raw
If I don't get my fingerprints
I have to call the Law

I touched you once too often
& I don't know who I am
My fingerprints were missing
When I wiped away the jam

I called my fingerprints all night
But they don't seem to care
The last time that I saw them
They were leafing through your hair

I thought I'd leave this morning
So I emptied out your drawer
A hundred thousand fingerprints
Floated to the floor

You hardly stooped to pick them up
You don't count what you lose
You don't even seem to know
Whose fingerprints are whose

When I had to say goodbye
You weren't there to find
You took my fingerprints away
So I would love your mind

I don't pretend to understand
Just what you mean by that

But next time I'll inquire
Before I scratch your back

I wonder if my fingerprints
Get lonely in the crowd
There are no others like them
& that should make them proud

Now you want to marry me
& take me down the aisle
& throw confetti fingerprints
You know that's not my style

Sure I'd like to marry
But I won't face the dawn
With any girl who knew me
When my fingerprints were on

1966

FOREIGN GOD, REIGNING
IN EARTHLY GLORY . . .

Foreign God, reigning in earthly glory between the Godless God and this greedy telescope of mine: touch my hidden jelly muscle, ring me with some power, I must conquer Babylon and New York. Draw me with a valuable sign, raise me to your height. You and I, dear Foreign God, we both are demons who must disappear in the perpetual crawling light, the fumbling sparks printing the shape of each tired form. We must be lost soon in the elementary Kodak experiment, in the paltry glory beyond our glory, the chalk-squeak of our most limitless delight. We are devoted yokels of the mothy parachute, the salvation of ordeal, we paid good money for the perfect holy scab, the pilgrim kneecap, the shoulder freakish under burden, the triumphant snow-man who does not freeze. Down with your angels, Foreign God, down with us, adepts of magic: into the muddy fire of our furthest passionate park, let us consign ourselves now, puddles, peep-holes, dreary oceanic pomp seen through the right end of the telescope, the minor burn, the kingsize ciga-rette, the alibi atomic holocaust, let us consign ourselves to the unmeasured exile outside the rules of lawlessness. O God, in thy foreign or godless form, in thy form of illusion or with the ringscape of your lethal thumb, you stop direc-tion, you crush this down, you abandon the evidence you pressed on its tongue.

1965

I BELIEVE YOU HEARD YOUR
MASTER SING

I believe you heard your master sing
while I lay sick in bed
I believe he told you everything
I keep locked in my head
Your master took you traveling
at least that's what you said
O love did you come back to bring
your prisoner wine and bread

You met him at some temple where
they take your clothes at the door
He was just a numberless man of a pair
who has just come back from the war
You wrap his quiet face in your hair
and he hands you the apple core
and he touches your mouth now so suddenly bare
of the kisses you had on before

He gave you a German shepherd to walk
with a collar of leather and nails
He never once made you explain or talk
about all of the little details
such as who had a worm and who had a rock
and who had you through the mails
Your love is a secret all over the block
and it never stops when he fails

He took you on his air-o-plane
which he flew without any hands
and you cruised above the ribbons of rain
that drove the crowd from the stands

Then he killed the lights on a lonely lane
where an ape with angel glands
erased the final wisps of pain
with the music of rubber bands

And now I hear your master sing
You pray for him to come
His body is a golden string
that your body is hanging from
His body is a golden string
My body is growing numb
O love I hear your master sing
Your shirt is all undone

Will you kneel beside the bed
we polished long ago
before your master chose instead
to make my bed of snow
Your hair is wild your knuckles red
and you're speaking much too low
I can't make out what your master said
before he made you go

I think you're playing far too rough
For a lady who's been to the moon
I've lain by the window long enough
(you get used to an empty room)
Your love is some dust in an old man's cuff
who is tapping his foot to a tune
and your thighs are a ruin and you want too much
Let's say you came back too soon

I loved your master perfectly
I taught him all he knew

He was starving in a mystery
like a man who is sure what is true
I sent you to him with my guarantee
I could teach him something new
I taught him how you would long for me
No matter what he said no matter what you do

THIS MORNING I WAS DRESSED BY THE WIND

This morning I was dressed by the wind.
The sky said, close your eyes and run
this happy face into a sundrift.
The forest said, never mind, I am as old
as an emerald, walk into me gossiping.
The village said, I am perfect and intricate,
would you like to start right away?
My darling said, I am washing my hair in the water
we caught last year, it tastes of stone.
This morning I was dressed by the wind,
it was the middle of September in 1965.

I STEPPED INTO AN AVALANCHE

I stepped into an avalanche
It covered up my soul
When I am not a hunchback
I sleep beneath a hill
You who wish to conquer pain
Must learn to serve me well

You strike my side by accident
As you go down for gold
The cripple that you clothe and feed
is neither starved nor cold
I do not beg for company
in the centre of the world

When I am on a pedestal
you did not raise me there
your laws do not compel me
to kneel grotesque and bare
I myself am pedestal
for the thing at which you stare

You who wish to conquer pain
must learn what makes me kind
The crumbs of love you offer me
are the crumbs I've left behind
Your pain is no credential
It is the shadow of my wound

I have begun to claim you
I who have no greed
I have begun to long for you
I who have no need

The avalanche you're knocking at
is uninhabited

Do not dress in rags for me
I know you are not poor
Don't love me so fiercely
when you know you are not sure
It is your world beloved
It is your flesh I wear

V / New Poems

THIS IS FOR YOU

This is for you
it is my full heart
it is the book I meant to read you
when we were old
Now I am a shadow
I am restless as an empire
You are the woman
who released me
I saw you watching the moon
you did not hesitate
to love me with it
I saw you honouring the windflowers
caught in the rocks
you loved me with them
On the smooth sand
between pebbles and shoreline
you welcomed me into the circle
more than a guest
All this happened
in the truth of time
in the truth of flesh
I saw you with a child
you brought me to his perfume
and his visions
without demand of blood
On so many wooden tables
adorned with food and candles
a thousand sacraments
which you carried in your basket
I visited my clay
I visited my birth
until I became small enough

and frightened enough
to be born again
I wanted you for your beauty
you gave me more than yourself
you shared your beauty
this I only learned tonight
as I recall the mirrors
you walked away from
after you had given them
whatever they claimed
for my initiation
Now I am a shadow
I long for the boundaries
of my wandering
and I move
with the energy of your prayer
and I move
in the direction of your prayer
for you are kneeling
like a bouquet
in a cave of bone
behind my forehead
and I move toward a love
you have dreamed for me

YOU DO NOT HAVE TO LOVE ME

You do not have to love me
just because
you are all the women
I have ever wanted
I was born to follow you
every night
while I am still
the many men who love you

I meet you at a table
I take your fist between my hands
in a solemn taxi
I wake up alone
my hand on your absence
in Hotel Discipline

I wrote all these songs for you
I burned red and black candles
shaped like a man and a woman
I married the smoke
of two pyramids of sandalwood
I prayed for you
I prayed that you would love me
and that you would not love me

IT'S JUST A CITY, DARLING

It's just a city, darling,
      everyone calls New York.
Wherever it is we meet
      I can't go very far from.
I can't connect you with
      anything but myself.
Half of the wharf is bleeding.
I'd give up anything to love you
      and I don't even know what the list is
but one look into it
      demoralizes me like a lecture.
If we are training each other for another love
      what is it?
I only have a hunch
      in what I've become expert.
Half of the wharf is bleeding,
it's the half where we always sleep.

EDMONTON, ALBERTA,
DECEMBER 1966, 4 A.M.

Edmonton, Alberta, December 1966, 4 a.m.
When did I stop writing you?
The sandalwood is on fire in this small hotel on Jasper
    Street.
You've entered the room a hundred times
disguises of sari and armour and jeans,
and you sit beside me for hours
like a woman alone in a happy room.
I've sung to a thousand people
and I've written a small new song
I believe I will trust myself with the care of my soul.
I hope you have money for the winter.
I'll send you some as soon as I'm paid.
Grass and honey, the singing radiator,
the shadow of bridges on the ice
of the North Saskatchewan River,
the cold blue hospital of the sky—
it all keeps us such sweet company.

THE BROOM IS AN ARMY OF STRAW

The broom is an army of straw
or an automatic guitar,
The dust absorbs a changing chord
that the yawning dog can hear,
My truces have retired me
and the truces are at war.
Is this the house, Beloved,
is this the window sill where
I meet you face to face?
Are these the rooms, are these the walls,
is this the house that opens on the world?
Have you been loved in this disguise
too many times, ring of powder left behind
by teachers polishing their ecstasy?
Beloved of empty spaces
there is dew on the mirror:
can it nourish the bodies in the avalanche
the silver could not exhume?
Beloved of war,
am I obedient to a tune?
Beloved of my injustice,
is there anything to be won?
Summon me as I summon from this house
the mysteries of death and use.
Forgive me the claims I embrace.
Forgive me the claims I renounce.

I MET YOU

I met you
just after death
had become truly sweet
There you were
24 years old
Joan of Arc
I came after you
with all my art
with everything
you know I am a god
who needs to use your body
who needs to use your body
to sing about beauty
in a way no one
has ever sung before
you are mine
you are one of my last women

CALM, ALONE,
THE CEDAR GUITAR

Calm, alone, the cedar guitar
tuned into a sunlight drone,
I'm here with sandalwood
and Patricia's clove pomander.
Thin snow carpets
on the roofs of Edmonton cars
prophesy the wilderness to come.
Downstairs in Swan's Café
the Indian girls are hunting
with their English names.
In Terry's Diner the counter man
plunges his tattoo in soapy water.
Don't fall asleep until your plan
includes every angry nomad.
The juke-box sings of service everywhere
while I work to renew the style
which models the apostles
on these friends whom I have known.

YOU LIVE LIKE A GOD

You live like a god
somewhere behind the names
I have for you,
your body made of nets
my shadow's tangled in,
your voice perfect and imperfect
like oracle petals
in a herd of daisies.
You honour your own god
with mist and avalanche
but all I have
is your religion of no promises
and monuments falling
like stars on a field
where you said you never slept.
Shaping your fingernails
with a razorblade
and reading the work
like a Book of Proverbs
no man will ever write for you,
a discarded membrane
of the voice you use
to wrap your silence in
drifts down the gravity between us,
and some machinery
of our daily life
prints an ordinary question in it
like the Lord's Prayer raised
on a rollered penny.
Even before I begin to answer you
I know you won't be listening.
We're together in a room,

it's an evening in October,
no one is writing our history.
Whoever holds us here in the midst of a Law,
I hear him now
I hear him breathing
as he embroiders gorgeously our simple chains.

AREN'T YOU TIRED

Aren't you tired
of your beauty tonight
How can you carry your burden
under the stars
Just your hair
just your lips
enough to crush you
Can you see where I'm running
the heavy *New York Times*
with your picture in it
somewhere in it
somewhere in it
under my arm

SHE SINGS SO NICE

She sings so nice
there's no desire in her voice
She sings alone
to tell us all
that we have not been found

THE REASON I WRITE

The reason I write
is to make something
as beautiful as you are

When I'm with you
I want to be the kind of hero
I wanted to be
when I was seven years old
a perfect man
who kills

WHEN I MEET YOU IN THE SMALL STREETS

When I meet you in the small streets
of rain-streaked movies
and old-fashioned shaving equipment,
you smile at me from my blood, saying:
an obsolete wisdom would have married us
when I was fourteen, O my teacher.
   I walk through your Moorish eyes
into sun and mathematics. I polish
Holland diamonds, and deep into Russia
I codify in one laser verse the haphazard
numbers leaping from each triangular story—
oh all world-hated flashing work
I make precise
for the sake of the perfect world.

Like jigsaw pieces married too early
in the puzzle we are pried apart
for every new experiment, as if simplicity
and good luck were not enough to build
a rainbow through gravity and mist.

IT HAS BEEN SOME TIME

It has been some time
since I took away
a woman's perfume on my skin
I remember tonight
how sweet I used to find it
and tonight I've forgotten nothing
of how little it means to me
knowing in my heart
we would never be lovers
thinking much more about suicide and money

A PERSON WHO EATS MEAT

A person who eats meat
wants to get his teeth into something
A person who does not eat meat
wants to get his teeth into something else
If these thoughts interest you for even a moment
you are lost

Who will finally say
you are perfect
Who will choose you
in order to edit your secrets

I sing this for your children
I sing this for the crickets
I sing this for the army
for all who do not need me

Whom will you address
first thing tomorrow morning
your dreams so bureaucratic
you refuse to appear in them

How beautiful the solemn are
Yes I have noticed you
Whoever gives you money
will be remembered for his pride

I love to speak to you this way
knowing how you came to me
leaving everything unsaid
that might employ us

When you are torn
when your silver is torn
take down this book and find
your place in my head

WAITING TO TELL THE DOCTOR

Waiting to tell the doctor
that he failed
and that I failed
I count the few remaining coins
I should have dropped at Monte Carlo
in the little wishing well
they offer you with the gun

still thinking about you
and the sparks between us
dull, milky and peculiar now
like dimes that have been dipped
in mercury too long ago

Last night I asked my brain
to put back into my loins
my love for you
Free at last I fell asleep
both of us naked and hungry
I am sure you willed me
the fullest audience with your body
on condition I die

What did you leave in my room
on my bed
against the wall
that is so cold and impossible and greedy

It's good to sit with people
    who are up so late
your other homes wash away
and other meals you left
    unfinished on the plate
It's just coffee
    and a piano player's cigarette
and Tim Hardin's song
and the song in your head
    that always makes you wait
I'm thinking of you
      little Frédérique
with your white white skin
and your stories of wealth
    in Normandy
I don't think I ever told you
that I wanted to save the world
watching television
     while we made love
ordering Greek wine and olives for you
while my friend scattered
dollar bills over the head
of the belly-dancer
under the clarinettes of Eighth Avenue
listening to your plans
for an exclusive pet shop in Paris
    Your mother telephoned me
she said I was too old for you
and I agreed
but you came to my room
one morning after a long time
because you said you loved me

From time to time I meet men
who said they gave you money
and some girls have said
that you weren't really a model
Don't they know what it means
to be lonely
lonely for boiled eggs in silver cups
lonely for a large dog
who obeys your voice
lonely for rain in Normandy
seen through leaded windows
lonely for a fast car
lonely for restaurant asparagus
lonely for a simple prince
and an explorer
I'm sure they know
but we are all creatures of envy
we need our stone fingernails
on another's beauty
we demand the hidden love
of everyone we meet
the hidden love not the daily love

Your breasts are beautiful
warm porcelain taste
of worship and greed

Your eyes come to me
under the perfect spikes
of imperishable eyelashes

Your mouth living
on French words
and the soft ashes of your make-up
Only with you

I did not imitate myself
only with you

I asked for nothing
your long long fingers
deciphering your hair
    your lace blouse
borrowed from a photographer
the bathroom lights
flashing on your new red fingernails
your tall legs at attention
    as I watch you from my bed
while you brush dew
        from the mirror
to work behind the enemy lines
      of your masterpiece
Come to me if you grow old
come to me if you need coffee

DO NOT FORGET OLD FRIENDS

Do not forget old friends
you knew long before I met you
the times I know nothing about
being someone
who lives by himself
and only visits you on a raid

MARITA

MARITA
PLEASE FIND ME
I AM ALMOST 30

HE STUDIES TO DESCRIBE

He studies to describe
the lover he cannot become
failing the widest dreams of the mind
& settling for visions of God

The tatters of his discipline
have no beauty
that he can hold so easily
      as your beauty

He does not know how
to trade himself for your love
Do not trust him
unless you love him

INDEX OF FIRST LINES

A cloud of grasshoppers,   *48*
A cross didn't fall on me,   *182*
A kite is a victim you are sure of,   *37*
A person who eats meat,   *233*
Aren't you tired,   *230*
As I lay dead,   *57*
As the mist leaves no scar,   *63*

Beneath my hands,   *62*
Beside the shepherd dreams the beast,   *33*
Between the mountains of spices,   *73*

Calm, alone, the cedar guitar,   *228*
Catching winter in their carved nostrils,   *7*
Claim me, blood, if you have a story,   *203*
Clean as the grass from which,   *186*
Come back to me,   *178*
Come, my brothers,   *104*
Come upon this heap,   *99*
Created fires I cannot love,   *202*

Do not arrange your bright flesh in the sun,   *29*
Do not forget old friends,   *238*
During the first pogrom they,   *13*

Edmonton, Alberta, December 1966, 4 a.m.,   *225*
Evidently they need a lot . . . ,   *118*
Eyes: . . . . . . Medium,   *122*

Finally I called the people I didn't want to hear from,   *103*
Flowers for Hitler the summer yawned,   *134*
For a lovely instant I thought she would grow mad,   *9*
For you,   *76*
For your sake I said I will praise the moon,   *52*
Foreign God, reigning in earthly glory,   *213*
Found once again shamelessly ignoring . . . ,   *193*

Give me back my fingerprints,   *211*
Give me back my house,   *171*
Go by brooks, love,   *43*

God, God, God, someone of my family,   72

He has returned from countless wars,   8
He pulled a flower,   22
He studies to describe,   239
He was beautiful when he sat alone, he was like me,
    he had,   205
He was lame,   195
He was wearing a black moustache and leather hair,   126
Here we are at the window . . . ,   185
His blood on my arm is warm as a bird,   4
His last love poem,   97
His pain, unowned, he left,   102
Hitler the brain-mole looks out of my eyes,   98
How you murdered your family,   16
Hurt once and for all into silence,   44

I almost went to bed,   68
I am a priest of God,   207
I am locked in a very expensive suit,   90
I am one of those who could tell . . . ,   78
I am sorry that the rich man must go,   168
I am too loud when you are gone,   195
I ask you where you want to go,   130
I believe you heard your master sing,   214
I don't believe the radio stations,   95
I do not know if the world has lied,   87
I had it for a moment,   135
I have not lingered in European monasteries,   45
I have two bars of soap,   60
I heard of a man,   30
I long to hold some lady,   64
I met a woman long ago,   198
I met you,   227
I once believed a single line,   124
I see you on a Greek mattress,   188
I stepped into an avalanche,   217
I want your warm body to disappear,   142
I was the last passenger of the day,   128
I wonder how many people in this city,   42
I would like to remind,   167

If I had a shining head,   12
If this looks like a poem,   56
If your neighbor disappears,   31
In almond trees lemon trees,   208
In his black armour,   30
In many movies I came upon an idol,   140
In the Bible generations pass . . . ,   192
Is there anything emptier,   89
It has been some time,   233
It's good to sit with people,   236
It's just a city, darling,   224
It's so simple,   114
It swings, Jocko,   46
I've seen some lonely history,   200

January 28 1962,   91

Layton, when we dance our freilach,   69
Listen all you bullets,   173
Listen to the stories,   93
Loving you, flesh to flesh, I often thought,   59

MARITA,   239
Martha they say you are gentle,   100
My friend walks through our city this winter night,   176
My lady can sleep,   58
My lady was found mutilated,   26
My love, the song is less than sung,   54
My lover Peterson,   20
My rabbi has a silver buddha,   116

Nothing has been broken,   184

One night I burned the house I loved,   190
Out of some simple part of me,   111
Out of the land of heaven,   71

Poems! break out!   113

Queen Victoria,   142

Several faiths,   *132*
She sings so nice,   *231*
She tells me a child built her house,   *32*
Silence,   *70*
Snow is falling,   *201*
So you're the kind of vegetarian,   *183*
Somewhere in my trophy room . . . ,   *196*
Strafed by the Milky Way,   *139*
Suzanne takes you down,   *209*
Suzanne wears a leather coat,   *189*

The big world will find out,   *174*
The broom is an army of straw,   *226*
The coherent statement was made,   *131*
The day wasn't exactly my own,   *88*
The famous doctor held up Grandma's stomach,   *92*
The flowers that I left in the ground,   *38*
The miracle we all are waiting for,   *134*
The moon dangling wet like a half-plucked eye,   *28*
The naked weeping girl,   *11*
The nightmares do not suddenly,   *181*
The pain-monger came home,   *115*
The reason I write,   *231*
The snow was falling,   *175*
The stony path coiled around me,   *119*
The sun is tangled,   *21*
The torture scene developed under a glass bell,   *117*
The warrior boats from Portugal,   *14*
There are some men,   *40*
This could be my little,   *106*
This is for you,   *221*
This morning I was dressed by the wind,   *216*
Those unshadowed figures, rounded lines of men,   *5*
Tonight I will live with my new white skin,   *137*
Toronto has been good to me,   *164*
Towering black nuns frighten us,   *24*
Two hours off the branch and burnt,   *138*
Two went to sleep,   *191*

Under her grandmother's patchwork quilt,   *65*

Waiting to tell the doctor,   235
We meet at a hotel,   129
Whatever cities are brought down,   41
When I hear you sing,   194
When I meet you in the small streets,   232
When I paid the sun to run,   187
When this American woman,   10
When we learned that his father . . . ,   123
When with lust I am smitten,   67
When you kneel below me,   61
When young the Christians told me,   3
Who is purer,   108
Who will finally say,   234
With all Greek heroes,   18
With Annie gone,   68

You dance on the day you saved,   172
You do not have to love me,   223
You have the lovers,   50
You know where I have been,   197
You live like a god,   229
You recited the Code of Comparisons,   165
You tell me that silence,   39